WIN OR DIE

"It was the movement that first attracted him – he could not hear a sound from this distance, but the sudden realisation of what must be happening sent a cold chill of horror through him. The flashing up-and-down movement of the cavalrymen's swords made the killing group look like some huge, evil, many-armed monster. The icy chill the King had felt was replaced by a sudden flush of heat all over the surface of his skin. His scalp crawled with furious anger mingled suddenly with fear for his own safety . . ."

ABOUT THE AUTHOR

Rolf Harris was born in Perth, Western
Australia. He's lived in England for over
thirty years now but spends a great deal of
each year in his native Australia. He travels
extensively and is known and loved
throughout the world as a musician, singer,
writer, entertainer and artist.

His best-selling books *Your Cartoon Time*
and *A Catalogue of Comic Verse* are also
available from Knight Books.

THE MAKING OF A KING

Written and illustrated by
Rolf Harris

KNIGHT BOOKS
Hodder and Stoughton

First published in Great Britain in
1989 simultaneously by Hodder
and Stoughton Children's Books
and Knight Books

British Library C.I.P.

Harris, Rolf
  Win or die.
  I. Title
  823 [J]

ISBN 0-340-51617-8

Printed and bound in Great Britain
for Hodder and Stoughton
Paperbacks, a division of Hodder and
Stoughton Ltd, Mill Road, Dunton
Green, Sevenoaks, Kent TN13 2YA.
(Editorial Office: 47 Bedford Square,
London WC1B 3DP)
by Richard Clay Ltd, Bungay, Suffolk

Acknowledgements

Thanks to my dearest Alwen, who puts up with my untidiness and disorganisation. Without your help and total support, nothing that I do would be possible at all.

Thanks to Tim Witney who carries on his father's interest and enthusiasm for bees and filled me in on all the things I didn't know about working in harmony with these fascinating creatures.

Thanks to Joanna Witney, now Mrs Osman, of Angel Farm Pottery, for all the freely given technical assistance and information about pottery making.

Thanks to Elsa Petersen-Schepelern of Hodder and Stoughton in Australia who steered me towards a friend of hers from university days who, as she said, might be able to help me with some background information on fencing.

Thanks to Lachie Hill, that friend, fencing enthusiast and one time captain of her university's fencing team. She started off trying to explain to me what it would be like for a complete novice like myself to attempt to learn to swordfight seriously. Eventually, after a huge amount of initial information which I tried to assimilate she steered me towards someone she felt was better qualified to help.

Thanks to Patrick Morley, that someone, President of the Cyrano Fencing Club of New South Wales. He vetted my first swordfighting scenes of the book and gave invaluable help, proof-reading and correcting, and often suggesting directions in which the story might go to achieve authenticity.

Thanks to Patrick's daughter, Rachel, who took me along to a club practice session where I saw my first fencing displays from her and other club members and actually watched at close quarters a visiting expert from China taking a young lad in his very first lesson. It was exactly what I wanted. I got into conversation there with Rowan Turner, who was waiting for his turn to fence. He expressed interest in the rough story line but said it could never work in the time frame I had planned, unless the King had a couple of real swordfights on the way to his confrontation with the Count.

It was his suggestion that the King should get out of trouble the first time more by luck than by good management (that was how Malgordo came into the story) and that the second occasion should be a fight to the death where the King could try out his 'secret move' successfully (the attack by the robbers).

Thanks to Rohan.

Thanks to Clifton Pugh for inviting me to his home in Victoria to do the illustrations. It was marvellous to have the artistic atmosphere all around me that week and to have the benefit of Cliff's constructive comments all along the way.

Thanks to his artist neighbour Rick Amor, who happily posed for the various pictures of Gordo.

Thanks to my Uncle Olaf Harris, back in Sydney, who was an ideal Silvander the Potter, and thanks to Patrick Morley's older daughter Rebecca, herself an accomplished fencer, who modelled for Lissia, the Potter's daughter.

Thanks to my drummer mate, Keith Harrison, who was the model for old Roger (sorry I had to age you so much in the drawing process, Keith!).

Thanks to Ansett air hostess Sonya Bell, who was just perfect for Queen Alice.

Thanks to Alistaire Caine and Mark Ward, both from Berkshire in the U.K., who were the models for the King and Turon respectively.

Last but not least thanks are certainly due to Ansett Airlines of Australia and N.E.C. As I wrote my book in longhand while travelling all around Australia doing concerts, I would send twenty and thirty odd pages at a time, free of charge, using the N.E.C. Fax facility in Ansett's Golden Wing lounges. These would magically appear at the same instant at my publisher's in London. They are almost sure that it is the first book to be sent in total in this way.

Thanks again.

Rolf Harris
September 1989

1

Alonzo felt as if he had been slapped across the face. He could feel himself blushing.

"You ask anybody," the old beekeeper said, "the new King's rubbish – although I daren't say that when anyone's listening, anyone important, that is. I'd be put inside in the blink of an eye. No . . . he's useless. He's doubled and trebled the taxes on everything and —"

"He's done no such thing!" Alonzo cut across the old man's words, and then, realising he must be more careful, he lowered the tone of his voice and said, "Well, not that I've heard."

"You wouldn't, young sir, not unless you was trying to make an honest living. But take my word for it, he's killing trade, changing our old money for all this new fangled stuff! No one trusts the paper notes – they want coins in their pockets. That's why we've returned to bartering."

Alonzo stood there smarting at the injustice of it all. He had *not* increased taxes. He would dearly love to explain, but he knew that he dare not reveal his identity, even to this apparently harmless old man. Count Tzlenko had warned him that he was not popular with the people, and that all sorts of secret gangs of malcontents were roaming the countryside and would harm him if they found him alone.

Alonzo swallowed his hurt pride and, smoothing the ridiculous wig down around his ears, he tried to start again in a normal voice.

"Well, if you won't take my money, I'm afraid I cannot take your honey," he smiled, almost laughed. "That rhymes . . . sorry . . . what was I saying? Oh yes, I can't pay you, I just can't take the honey."

"Young sir, as I said, we've all gone back to barter, well, a lot of us have." The old man looked pointedly at Alonzo, waiting for an answer.

"But I've nothing to barter with," Alonzo said.

The old man's eyes shifted upwards until he was looking at the top of Alonzo's head and, stroking his hands over his own balding dome, he said, "Begging your pardon, young sir, but that wig you're wearing . . ." The old man ignored Alonzo's frowning face and the words tumbled out. "It's a lovely wig, sir, beautifully made. I've always wanted to be able to afford such a thing. I wouldn't mind having that wig, young sir, and if you should feel that the honey was worth it . . . I . . . er . . ."

Alonzo couldn't believe it. The old beekeeper had wiped his nose on the sleeve of his shirt and was trying to disguise the fact that his eyes had filled with tears. All at once Alonzo felt guilty at taking everything for granted, for assuming that the old man was dressed so lightly by choice on this fairly chilly day. It was a shock to realise that if the old man couldn't afford a wig, he almost certainly couldn't afford a warm jacket either. Alonzo snatched the wig from his head and laughing to

8

cover his embarrassment, passed it to the old man.

How good it was to feel the freedom of his hair once again hanging halfway down to his shoulders instead of being bunched up and hot under the wig. He realised in horror that the old man was now openly crying – clutching the wig to his chest with both hands, as the tears rolled unchecked down his cheeks.

"Don't say anything," said Alonzo. "Wrap this around you, you're shivering." He dragged off the patched peasant jacket with a certain amount of relief. He had never liked the rough feel of it and he draped it around the frail shoulders. "Look, I really must be going," he continued, and bending down to pick up the sack with the jars inside, he muttered, "Thanks once again for the honey and for telling me all about your bees."

The old man gave a loud sniff and dried his eyes on

the jacket sleeve. "It's been a pleasure meeting you today. I've never had anyone so interested in my bees. You've got a real feeling for them. Come back any time, young sir. Oh look, I never thought, I can show you a short cut . . . save you best part of a league."

He refused to take "no" for an answer, and in a short time the two of them had walked some way back down the road towards the capital and the old man was pointing out the almost overgrown entrance to a footpath. It cut down through what had once obviously been a fairly grand formal garden. Huge flowering shrubs ran wild there, providing an almost impenetrable curtain of greenery.

"Just follow what's left of the path, young sir. It goes down past the ruins of the old house. Did I tell you, I was an apprentice gardener's lad there? No, well, that was a long time ago – where was I?"

"The ruins," Alonzo started to say.

"Ah, yes, go right around the ruins of the old house and the path divides into three. You take the left-hand bit and go right on through the woods and you meet this road as it loops all the way back round the hillside. It's a bit tricky at the end. You've got quite a steep climb up to the road, but it does save you a good deal of walking. Luck be with you, then – come back and see me – bring me a different coloured wig I can wear for Sundays." He burst into a cackle of laughter and the King laughed self-consciously, feeling his cheeks flushing scarlet once again. He'd never explained why he had worn the wig, and really couldn't do so without telling the old man who he really was. He made his farewell in a slightly embarrassed way, and set off.

He had walked for quite a while and was rather enjoying the feeling of strain on the backs of his legs from the path's downhill slope when a sudden flash of light from the corner of his vision made him turn his head. He stopped and looked up to the tangled trees that shut off his view of the distant roadway and there it was again, another flash of light. A faint far-off jingling came to his ears and he realised that it must be some rider, or riders.

He moved back up a few paces until he could see a clear patch through the trees and was amazed and then very relieved to recognise the black and silver livery. The riders were from Count Tzlenko's crack bodyguard. "What are *they* doing here?" he wondered, and then realised it was a great stroke of good fortune for him. He'd never *met* any of the guard, but it would be a simple, safe matter for him to reveal himself to them as their King. He could easily double up with one of the mounted bodyguard. It would certainly save him a long walk back to the capital. He called out as loudly as he could. There was no response. "Too far away," he muttered, and set off running back the way he had come. As he ran he found himself wishing he knew the name of the captain of the guard. It would make the formal meeting so much easier.

It was a lot harder climbing back up the path than it had been coming down, and soon he was gasping for breath. He stopped, hot and exhausted, the sweat trickling down his back under the shirt, his forehead and cheeks shiny with exertion. Finally he burst up out of the bushes back onto the road, but was unable to stop himself from pitching forward onto his hands and knees.

It was an awkward fall. He was trying to protect the jars of honey and took most of his weight on the palm of his left hand. Both of his knees felt grazed and when he lifted up his hand all the skin on his palm was broken and bleeding. His feeling of self-pity was so strong that he was not immediately aware of what was happening away to his right in the direction of the old beekeeper's hut.

It was the movement that first attracted him – he could not hear a sound from this distance, but the sudden realisation of what must be happening sent a cold chill of horror through him. The flashing up-and-down movement of the cavalrymen's swords made the killing group look like some huge, evil, many-armed monster. The icy chill the King had felt was replaced by a sudden flush of heat all over the surface of his skin. His scalp crawled with furious anger mingled suddenly with fear for his own safety.

He scrabbled backwards and crawled into the screen of bushes, dragging the branches back to cover any sign of his entrance. He was so tired that he was shaking, but every now and again, he found himself holding his breath so that he should hear the horsemen if they started to return.

His brain was racing furiously to try and make some sense out of what he had seen. "It must be the old man," he thought. "But why? What's he done? Could he be a spy? That's rubbish! *Why?*" he cried out loud and then clapped his hand over his mouth and crouched down further as he heard the faint jingle of harness approaching from his right.

He glanced back and froze in horror. He could quite clearly see the marks in the roadway where he'd fallen and the line in the dust where he had dragged the honey – a straight arrow which seemed to be pointing directly to his hiding place. They would discover him easily.

But as the bodyguard approached, Alonzo realised that none of them was interested in searching for anyone. They sounded almost in party mood and were eagerly questioning the captain. All discipline was gone.

"Who was he?" one voice queried.

"Come on, you must know!" said another of the men. "He seemed such a harmless old rooster."

"Yes, well he won't cock-a-doodle-doo any more," said another, and great guffaws of laughter came from almost opposite the King's hiding place.

"Halt! Rest easy," said a voice of obvious authority. "Look, shut up the lot of you. Let's have a bit of silence and I'll tell you what little I know and then let that be an end of your questions, or you'll all be in a cell tonight instead of celebrating this miserable bit of sport."

The King tried to slow his breathing and strained to hear every word as the voice went on.

"Well, you all know the Count sent for me as soon as we returned from exercising the horses this morning. He was in a towering rage . . . some prisoner or other had escaped from the castle dungeon, although," the voice added as a sort of afterthought, "I can't see how anyone could escape from that hell-hole."

"Which prisoner was he?" came another voice.

"Hold your tongue! Do you think I was about to question the Count when he was in one of his rages? He dragged me down to a storeroom and showed me a peasant's coat which he said was identical with the one the prisoner had stolen except the other one had three

13

brown patches, one on the right shoulder and two on the . . . well, you know all that . . . that's how I knew it was him – that and the ginger wig the Count said he had got hold of as some form of disguise. I was to kill him on sight and not engage him in *any* conversation, as he was some kind of political prisoner. Anyway, you know the rest, how we followed him all through the markets and questioned everyone. He was a really weird escaped prisoner, I must say, made no attempt to hide himself – I suppose he never thought anyone would know of his disguise. Anyway, now you know as much as I do – the Count said there would be a special reward for all ten of us if we did find him and get rid of him. So that's it. No more questions. You know as much as I do, right? Let's have a bit of discipline or I'll have all your guts for girth straps."

There was a scattered laugh.

"Form loose threes. At the centre . . . ride . . . easy!" The horsemen moved away, chattering excitedly about the possible reward. Slowly the sounds of their going faded into silence and somewhere a bird started a short trilling call.

The King felt as if he had been poleaxed. To all outward appearances he crouched there as if in a daydream, but his brain was racing like some terrified runaway horse, his whole world overturned and smashed. The same three thoughts kept hammering in his head.

First, it was the Count who had insisted on him wearing that specific jacket with the brown patches. Secondly, it was the Count who had suggested the trip out to the markets in the first place. And lastly, it was the Count who had more or less forced him to wear the ghastly wig. Clearly Count Tzlenko had planned the brutal murder of the young King, and he had tricked his guards into carrying out that murder.

Alonzo carefully eased himself upright and crept to the edge of the road to look long and hard in each direction before he dared to come out into the open. No sign of the horsemen to the left. He turned and with a leaden, sick feeling in his stomach, he forced himself to walk towards the hut in the distance, and that awful bundle of what looked like old rags on the path leading up to the door.

2

The next three days were like a living nightmare. He had woken up well before dawn that first day and looked around uncomprehendingly in the gloom, trying to work out where he was. Hunger had woken him, but why was he so cold and uncomfortable?

The memory of the day before suddenly hit him. Somehow he had managed to bury the old beekeeper's body. He'd taken the jacket from the body and kept it for warmth, even though it was slashed and bloodied.

Alonzo was terrified – terrified first by what had happened, and second, by the thought that someone would come and find him. He had no right to be here in another man's home – even though it was such a rough, dismal place. He felt dreadfully guilty of . . . he knew not what . . . perhaps it was because the old man had been killed in mistake for him. He had begun imagining that a group of armed soldiers would suddenly spring out of ambush and attack him. Perhaps they were already in the hut? He could not quite make out the shapes of things in the darkened room – was there someone crouched in that far corner? He lay there almost afraid to breathe, his hand over his mouth to stop himself crying out. Slowly, when nothing happened, he relaxed. The pre-dawn light gradually built up outside and he was at last able to see clearly the few objects in the room and recognise them for what they were.

Once he had decided he was in no danger, he'd begun to search for something to eat. He opened one of the jars of honey he had bartered for, and using his fingers to scoop out the honey, wolfed down as much as he could. He searched the hut and finally found two apples, all wrinkled and old, lying in the corner of a box. He gobbled them down – the core, pips, everything. He smiled ruefully as he thought of his young wife in the Palace, just a few days ago, carefully peeling him an apple, and then cutting the remainder into quarters, removing the sections of the core before offering it to him. What wouldn't he give for that apple peel and those bits of core now?

To take his mind off his hunger, he set about exploring the surroundings of the hut. He knew the path to the row of beehives, or "houses" as the old man had called them, but he soon found that the other path led to a very primitive outhouse which stood over a huge hole dug in the ground, and the third lay in the opposite direction and took him first to a sort of cultivated garden area with some green-growing plants. He had no idea what they were.

He noticed that one part of the earth had been recently turned over, so he started on the next section and dug up one of the plants. Attached in places along the root of the plant were little round bits about as big as a decent-sized stone and they seemed to break off quite easily. He took a handful of them to the stream and washed the earth off them. He bit into one – it had a very sharp and unpalatable taste – certainly nothing to be eaten raw. His disappointment was intense. What was he going to do?

He lay down and drank deeply of the crystal clear water of the stream. How cold and sweet it tasted, he thought. His stomach was rumbling and churning for more to eat, but Alonzo didn't know how to find food. Should he try and head back to the capital? The very idea of that filled him with dread and immediately conjured up a superimposed hotchpotch of pictures of horsemen hacking with swords, pictures of the old man's body and the gaping wounds. He shuddered; he couldn't go back to the city, it would be madness, for in his mind he saw every man's sword against him.

Despair overtook him and he found himself once more hiding in terror inside the hut, listening for sounds of horses' hooves approaching. What *could* he do? As a lad he had never bothered with his lessons on swordsmanship – when would *he* ever need swordsmanship? He was the Prince, one day to be King. Why did *he* need to pay attention to the complicated exercises and moves of swordfighting – it was all too much like hard work. Now he found himself wishing, "If only I had listened . . ."

"If only" – they must be the most useless words in the language, Alonzo thought.

Once again he began to look around the hut. Trying to take his mind off the hunger pangs, he began to tidy up. There seemed to be pitifully few belongings. There was a fireplace and some wood, a couple of homemade candles, and some string and beeswax, obviously for making more candles. There was one big blackened pot and a hook which would suspend it over the fire (if he

20

could ever find out how to get a fire started), there were all bits and pieces of stones and sticks and dry grass in a small metal box off to one side of the room.

On the other side stood the rows of honey jars, all full, and all sealed around the top with beeswax. There was a large shapeless lump of the brown beeswax and some more bits of string. There were two of the honey jars standing empty at the end of the bottom row, and he wondered where the old man had got the jars from. He had obviously no means of making them in this little hut. Apart from a wolfskin, there was only the big old table with a full bucket of water standing by the leg.

Then, in the gloom of that one room, he noticed a three-legged stool pushed right back under the table, and as he reached in to get the stool, he noticed a drawer built into the underside of the table. This pulled out easily on waxed runners and inside he could see more bits of string and fragments of wax, as well as two knives, one with the blade almost sharpened away, an old spoon, a sort of dipper or ladle, a very old folding razor, and a square pottery bowl for holding salt.

The King could not believe that a person could live with so few things. There was absolutely nothing else in the room; no plates or cups or glasses, no wooden floors beneath his feet even, just hard, stamped-down earth. He looked again and saw that there seemed to be a slightly scooped out part of the table top which could be used, he supposed, as a sort of shallow dish.

The razor reminded him that his face felt itchy with two days' growth of beard, so he took the bucket of water and the razor outside where there was more light and set about shaving himself. The whole operation was a disaster. Firstly, he had never used a razor before – he had always been shaved by his own special valet. He had no mirror, and no idea how to hold the razor and on top of this he was terrified of cutting his face. The razor seemed to tug at his bristles and the pain of shaving in cold, latherless water was too much. He was on the point of giving up when he nicked his top lip just where it joined the nostril. He was furious with himself. He stormed back into the hut and slammed the closed razor back into the drawer.

The whole day was a disaster. He could not get away from the gnawing hunger pains in his stomach, but the thought of eating more honey made him feel sick. He explored the area on the other side of the little stream, but was afraid of getting lost in the forest beyond. He tried curling up on the wolfskin and going to sleep, but the hunger kept him awake, so eventually he wolfed down some more honey and felt dreadful. He drank quantities of water from the bucket to try and cut down on the sickly sweet taste of all the honey and eventually he had to rush outside and be sick. This left him shaky and empty and hungry and feeling really sorry for himself. He curled up again on the wolfskin and this time did manage to get to sleep, but in no time at all it seemed he was being woken by a furious banging. He staggered to the door and opened it and there stood a group of soldiers with swords drawn; and held between them was the ghastly body of the old beekeeper. They had obviously just dug him up because earth was clinging to his body. As the young King moved to brush away the earth, the dead eyelids jerked open and the eyes stared straight through him as both dead hands reached out to claw at his throat . . .

His terrified scream sat him bolt upright on the wolfskin, and he realised he'd been having a nightmare. It was so real that he could feel the claw-like hands around his throat still. His heart was hammering away at his ribs, and sweat was all over his face and hands.

Somehow two more days passed. The young King, afraid to go to sleep because of the terrible nightmares, seemed, to himself, to be on the verge of going mad, or of dying. He didn't ever want to taste honey again as long as he lived. In his far off Palace days he used to dream of a paradise in which he had endless supplies of honey, he loved it so much. The reality of having *only* honey to eat had changed his whole outlook. He felt dreadful. He was constantly scratching at his itchy new growth of stubble on his chin and the place where he had cut himself trying to shave would not seem to heal. He became progressively weaker and weaker, one time falling in and out of uneasy sleep, burning up with fever, and the next time waking up drenched with icy sweat from some dreadful nightmare, where more soldiers banged on more doors.

When on the morning of the fourth day, he woke from yet another nightmare to find that the banging was real, he was frozen with panic.

Voices called out, horse harness and metal work jingled, some heavy object battered the door and still he could not move. They had found him at last. Where could he run to? The voices called again – some from the back of the hut. This time he was trapped; there was nowhere to go.

Wearily the King dragged himself to his feet and feeling worse than he could ever remember feeling in his whole life, he stumbled to the door and lifted the wooden bar which held it closed.

He pushed open the door, narrowed his eyes as the sunlight flooded in to the gloom, and tried to prepare himself for death.

There was a swarthy young man standing there. He had long curling locks framing a smiling face. Behind him stood a highly decorated Romany caravan and four or five loose horses grazed at the edge of the road.

He looked back to the face of the young man to find that the smile had been replaced by a look of wariness and slight distaste. The light abruptly faded from the sky, and the scene in front of him seemed to perform a cartwheel as everything went black.

Alonzo woke slowly and the first thing he noticed was the light. There were several candles lit and a crackling sound turned his head. He stared in amazement at the fire in the blackened fireplace. "How did that happen?" he thought. "I don't know how to start a fire." The door opened and in came two men, one of them the man he had seen at the door. They were carrying a sort of over-stuffed lounge-chair between them. They dumped it down unceremoniously and both of them sat down on it.

"So you're awake!"

Alonzo looked again at the speaker and the memory of the banging on the door jerked back into his head. He must have fainted.

"What's the matter with you? Have you caught some sickness?"

"I'm just hungry," Alonzo said.

"What?" said the taller of the two and both of them burst out laughing. "Hungry? There's enough honey to last you a life-time. Potatoes out in the garden – a forest full of food – what's Grigori doing letting you get in this state? Where is the old man anyway?"

The King felt his eyes dropping away from the straightforward gaze of the Romany. He was breathing in a ragged, shallow sort of gasping way as he struggled up to a sitting position. He seemed to have to support his head in his hands. He couldn't think of anything to say.

At that moment, the back door was knocked open and three other men came in. One had backed in carrying a big pot which was half-full of water and one had taken off his coat and was using it as a sort of carrying bag for what the King now realised must be fresh young new potatoes, identical to the ones he had dug up and rejected.

There were also handfuls of nettles, little round cobnuts and a dozen or so big brown mushrooms.

"Can't find Grigori anywhere," said the third man, a much older man than the others. "He's not down talking to his beloved bees." He laughed but seeing his laugh was not echoed by the first two, he stopped.

"What's up?" he said.

An ominous silence filled the room. The coat, full of food, was dumped on the table and the five men stood in an accusing semi-circle around the wolfskin bed where Alonzo sat.

"You have some explaining to do."

When Alonzo said nothing, the first stranger stepped

across to stand right over him and said, "What's become of Grigori?"

There was a long silence.

"Grigori?" whispered Alonzo.

"Grigori, the beekeeper," said the man. "This is his hut. Where is he?"

"He's dead." Alonzo's body sagged. He buried his face in his hands.

"What?" The word cracked out like a cannon shot, and Alonzo felt himself grabbed by the shirt front and the lapel of the jacket, and jerked bodily to his feet.

"How? *How* is he dead?"

"Take your hands off me! How dare you!" The King was outraged. No one had ever manhandled him before.

The back-hand slap across the face felt as if it would take his head from his shoulders.

"That's how I dare," said the Romany, "why should I not dare, tell me, pray?" The look on his face told the King that this was no polite request. "Tell me!"

The King felt himself being shaken like a rag-doll.

"I am your King!" He screamed at the top of his voice. Even to himself he sounded like a petulant little boy having a temper tantrum. The others all burst into laughter and he felt himself dropped like some useless thing. He dragged himself up onto his hands and knees, but felt too weak and ashamed to look up. The laughter echoed all around him.

"I am your King," he repeated in a cracked whisper.

"Who are you? King Cockroach?" the youngest of the Romanies suggested, and the laughter started all over again. "King Cockroach. King Konstantin Cockroach, at your service, your Majesty!" The youngster made an exaggerated flourish with his hands and bowed low.

"Shut up!" The older man stepped forward. "Now then, listen, young man, these lies will do you no good. The King is dead. We all know that. What we want to know is what happened to Grigori."

"Leave it, Tomas." Although much younger, the other Romany was obviously the leader. The older man made a shrugging gesture, as if to say, "It's your problem", and stepped back, allowing the long-haired Romany to take charge. He stepped forward, squatted down on his haunches and looked very seriously at the King.

"I know you're sick," he said, "but you must tell us what you know of old Grigori. He was our friend. You said he was dead."

Alonzo nodded and the Romany continued.

"How do you know this?"

"I was the first to find him. I buried him," sobbed the King, and slipped down until his head was resting in his cupped hands.

"Where?"

"Just out there," the King nodded, indicating the direction with his head. A look from the leader and the youngest Romany slipped out through the door. As the door closed, the questioning started again.

"How did he die?"

The King did not know where to start explaining. Besides, there was something that was nagging away at him. He had to know. He indicated towards the older man. "He said you all know the King is dead."

"WHAT HAPPENED TO GRIGORI?" the leader shouted.

"You tell me about the King first, then I'll tell you!"

Crack! Another back-handed slap knocked his head sideways. He jerked into a defensive curled-up position, hiding his face. Eventually, between sobs, Alonzo poured out the tale as best he could. He told them of coming to buy honey, and of how well he had got on with the old man. He made no mention of wig or coat. How could he start to explain that side of it, if they wouldn't believe he was the King in the first place?

He got to the part about watching from his hiding place as the soldiers slew the kindly old man. He made no mention of recognising what group of soldiers they were. Then he stopped. He was thoroughly drained. The door opened and the young Romany came back in.

"There is a sort of grave out there," he said.

"Show me," said the leader, instantly on his feet. The two of them left the hut. The older man, Tomas, picked up the big pot of water and slung it on the hook over the fire. He shrugged.

"No use starving to death," he said. "While Orlo sorts it out, we'll get some food going here. Where did he keep his salt?"

He seemed to have directed the question to the King, but one of the other Romanies said, "Last time we were here he used it as a doorstop."

He went to the side of the door, stooped and picked up a square sort of brownish rock. "Still here." He went to the drawer in the table and taking out the thin knife, he started shaving into the pot a fine crystalline powder from the chunk of rock-salt. The potatoes and everything else went in and one of the Romanies was just picking up the ladle to do a bit of stirring when the one known as

Orlo put his head round the door and said, "Someone keep an eye on him, the rest of you, out here."

The others trooped out of the room, leaving Tomas to take up a sort of guarding position on the sofa. The King opened his mouth to ask a question, but all his resolve drained away as he looked at the cold expressionless face of the old man. His eyes flicked back to his hands and he marvelled at how they were shaking. He was *so* tired. If he just clenched his eyes shut again, he might wake in his bed in the Palace and laughingly explain to his young wife that he had just been having the most amusing nightmare. Tears began rolling down his cheeks but he wasn't aware of them – he was already asleep.

3

His nanny was feeding him the most delicious food he had ever tasted. He was a bit annoyed that she was holding the back of his head so firmly. He was a big boy now and could sit up without help. He tried to shake his head, or at least turn petulantly to one side – and that was when he woke up. He was being supported in a sitting position by Tomas, and being spoon-fed. The vegetable soup or stew, or whatever it was called, was exquisite.

Alonzo's stomach was growling with hunger as he gulped down as much as he could.

"Take it careful, lad, you'll need all your strength. We're taking you back with us."

It didn't sound too encouraging or cheerful.

"Taking me where? What do you mean?"

"Orlo's decided you must face the Council."

"What do you mean?" The King felt panicky.

"We've dug up the old man, and Orlo doesn't want to make a decision without the Council."

"I don't understand – decision on what?"

"Well, no one believes your story. We think you murdered Grigori. Either that or you're mad, and Orlo won't take the responsibility for your life so we're . . ."

Alonzo surged to his feet knocking the ladle out of the old man's hand.

"It's all true what I told you! I didn't kill the old man. I told you the truth!" he yelled, turning from one to the other of the unresponsive faces.

Orlo, the leader, stepped forward.

"Just be thankful I didn't pass judgement on you myself. I have been given the power. You are to be tried by the Shero Rom and the Council and . . ."

"I didn't touch the old man!" screamed the King. "Every word I told you is true!"

"You are still the King, are you?" Orlo's words were menacingly quiet.

"Yes! I am King Alonzo the Fourth and I demand that you . . ."

His words faltered to a frightened silence as he watched the quiet exchange of glances between the others, watched the slow, almost apologetic smile turning up one corner of Orlo's mouth. The smile did not reach the eyes which remained fixed on his face.

"The young King died of food poisoning in the Palace during a formal dinner honouring Count Tzlenko's bodyguard three days ago. Everyone at the banquet was struck down. Apart from the Count, the young Queen was the only one to come through it, and even now she still lies gravely ill. The Count, thinking it was the Bubonic plague, ordered the bodies to be instantly cremated. It was only when the Queen was examined later by the Count's physician that it was found to be food poisoning. The King's chef and his three kitchen assistants have been executed. All this we have from a proclamation from the Palace. And you claim, you still claim that you are the King?"

Alonzo shook his head in disbelief.

"Yes, no . . . I don't know what to say. All I know is that I have told you no lies. I have never found it necessary to lie." He could think of no argument that might help him now. There was a long silence, then, "Can I have some more to eat?" he said, in terrible despair.

The whole of the inside of the Romany caravan was crowded with all the stacked jars of honey from the hut, as well as all the empty pottery jars the Romanies had brought and were now taking back with them. Grigori's pitifully few belongings were there too, the big cooking pot still holding some soup. Alonzo's hands were tied behind him and then secured to one of the fixed uprights of the table in the corner.

The youngest Romany had been detailed to stay with Alonzo inside the caravan. It was his horse that was being used to carry the recently dug up body of the old man, and he was obviously fairly ill-at-ease from the moment he was left alone with the young King.

"My name is Turon," he said, "and I'm not supposed to talk to you, so you'd better not say anything. You hear me?"

When the King didn't answer, the young Romany got a bit flustered.

"Did you hear what I said?" he growled. The King did a sort of hunched shrug of his shoulders from this awkward position, and said, "You just told me I was not to say anything."

"Don't try to confuse me with your smart talk, King

Cockroach. I'm not supposed to talk to you at all." He nodded his head as if to say "I've won that argument", and silence reigned for quite a while.

Eventually the lack of talking seemed to get to the young lad and he volunteered some information about the pottery jars the King was looking at. "I did all the decoration on those. That was my idea to put all those curlicues round the lip like that. I like doing them." There was a lengthy pause, then, "I don't know what's going to happen with Grigori's bees. There was a long discussion while you were asleep. Orlando – that's his real name but everyone calls him Orlo except when his father, the Shero Rom's, around – Do you know anything about Romanies?"

Alonzo didn't want to stop the lad from talking so he just shook his head and said nothing.

"Well, the Shero Rom's like the King, except he's chosen by the Council of all the old men. They can dump him again if they lose faith in him, but that doesn't often happen. I've never heard of it happening anyway, but it could. Anyway, what was I talking about?"

"Orlando."

"Was I? Oh yes . . . Orlo was saying we should take all the beehives back with us now that Grigori's gone, but nobody's any good with bees. Everyone's scared of getting stung and Grigori says – used to say – that the bees smell your fear and they attack first. I don't believe it. We're going to miss his honey, though, when this lot's used up. We used to do a straight exchange – our pottery jars for his honey. Did I tell you I help make the pots? Oh yes, I told you that."

There was another very long silence.

"Did you really kill him?" The young Romany started up again.

The question brought the King back from his daydream. He shook his head sadly from side to side.

"Didn't kill him, huh! Tell me, King Konstantin Cockroach, why were you trying to kill yourself then, if you were not guilty? Eh? Tell me that!"

The King looked up. "What do you mean, trying to kill myself? I wasn't trying to kill myself!"

"You must have been. You were starving when we found you. There was Grigori's potato patch and a whole forest full of food. There was honey – you could have boiled up some soup and cooked all sorts of things."

"I don't even know how to make a fire," said the King.

"Ha!" Turon's laugh was part amusement, part disbelief. But as he looked at the straight face of the King, his smile gradually faded.

"You're serious, Konstantin? You really don't know how to make a fire? Did you try the tinder box?"

"What tinder box?" he muttered.

Turon was shaking his head from side to side. "I don't believe you." His voice cracked on the word "believe". "I don't believe . . . well, how did you . . . what did you do before? How did you live?"

"I *told* you," Alonzo yelled, to cover his embarrassment. "I'm the King. I never had to do anything! I never learnt how to do *anything*! I didn't have to because everything was done for me."

"Shut up in there!" Old Tomas's voice shouted back through the door. "Or I'll come in and bang your heads together!"

In the ensuing silence the two young men looked at each other.

"You really – I mean, *really* are the King?" the boy whispered.

"Yes, really! King Alonzo the Fourth."

Rather than grapple with the hard work involved in

this new lines of thinking, the lad went for a cheap laugh.

"I like King Konstantin Cockroach better," he said, and the mood of neutrality and approaching comradeship was broken.

4

His first view of the assembled Council filled Alonzo's heart with dread. There, off to the left, quite a way from them, was a rough trestle table on which the recently washed body of the old beekeeper lay. What was left of his shirt had been stripped away and the scraps of material lay under the table. The King suddenly realised that the sickly sweet smell must be coming from the body. He was hard-pressed to stop himself from being sick.

He looked away from the corpse to the group of old men who were about to decide whether he should live or die, and as he was marched closer, he tried in vain to find one friendly face among them. There were eighteen men apart from the chief, or as the Romanies called him, the Shero Rom. They all had their own chairs, some more ornate than others – some garishly painted – most of them carved in one way or another, and they were sitting in a curved line behind the Shero Rom. Every man was watching him as he approached, obviously trying to assess him and form some early opinion as to his guilt or innocence.

The King stopped in front of the assembled group and his two escorts stepped back a pace or two. He stood,

his eyes nervously darting from one face to another, acutely aware of how ragged he must look in his dirty peasant's clothes, with his face covered by four days' growth of beard.

"Could . . . er . . . could I have my hands untied?" he finally blurted out to the Shero Rom. He was amazed that he had been able to speak at all, his mouth was so dry with nervous tension.

"I'm sorry, young man, I should have seen to that a long time ago. It is not our intention to make you suffer needlessly."

The old man nodded his head and the two escorts busied themselves with the rope, finally untying him. The King chafed his hands and got the circulation going again.

"We want to find out the truth about Grigori," the

Shero Rom began. "He was our friend. Do you wish to speak first?"

Alonzo looked at the stern face of the Shero Rom and sensed a kindness behind the fierce front. He took a deep breath to steady himself and said, "Yes."

The Shero Rom nodded and addressing himself to the King and to the assembled members of the Council, he said, "My son has confessed himself puzzled and unsure as to how Grigori met his death. We have examined the wounds as best we could. There are many cuts, but other than that we can tell nothing. Speak!"

The King took a long breath, and launched into a detailed telling of everything he could remember of that fateful day. Was it only four days ago? He spared himself nothing, trying as best he could to list the things as they happened, including his feelings, his terrors, his sickness, and his inability to feed himself adequately. The only thing he held back was the fact that he was the King. Turon, the young Romany, had advised him against "blurting out all that King stuff", and maybe it *was* wiser, considering the bulletin which had been issued from the Palace. How could he hope to convince them in the face of such an official statement? He finally finished by explaining how he was woken by the Romanies and how he had fainted through lack of food and through relief from the terror of imagining himself about to be killed.

"And you never used your sword to attack Grigori?" the Shero Rom asked.

"I don't have a sword. I'm no good with a sword; I never learnt how to use one." Alonzo's voice became a bit of a gabble, as he realised that he was lying. He had about a dozen different swords: dress swords, a sword of State, a presentation sword, one of those new-fangled French rapiers, and an old pirate cutlass his father had given him – he had swords to burn back at the Palace. He looked at the old men and realised that most of them didn't believe him when he said he'd never learnt to use a sword. It was obviously part of every young man's education in the Romany camp to learn about swords and fighting.

"What did you do with your horse?"

"I don't have a horse!" Once again he thought of the choice of horses he had back at the Palace and he cursed his stupid face as he felt the blush starting to rise up into his cheeks.

"No sword and no horse?" The statement was a sort of question which obviously the Council found hard to swallow.

"I couldn't afford a horse." The King was now embarking on a course of deliberate lies. As he said it a small part of his mind said, "Stupid fool, you'll get found out!" But another part of his mind flashed up a picture of Turon saying, "They won't swallow any of that King rubbish, that's for sure." So that was what he was doing. He was avoiding telling them anything about being the King. It would be all right. He swallowed nervously.

"Can you ride a horse?" The Shero Rom's voice was quiet.

"Yes," Alonzo replied.

"And how do you explain that you can ride a horse, but you don't have a horse to ride?"

"I . . . er . . . " Alonzo was blushing again. "I learnt

from my father when I was small, but when my father died . . . er . . . his horse had to be sold."

There was a very long pause and every eye seemed to be boring holes right through him.

The Shero Rom cleared his throat and said, "You say a group of horsemen hacked Grigori to pieces. Why do you think they did this?"

"They may have mistaken . . . " The King faltered. If he kept on with this line of statement he would mention the wig and jacket and then the fact that he was King and had been out in disguise. ". . . Perhaps they thought he was someone else," he finished lamely.

"Does any of the Council wish to question this young man?"

No one spoke, so the Shero Rom turned back and called out, "Send for my son."

Cries of "Orlando, get Orlando" soon had the handsome young Romany striding in through the tent flap and across to stand in front of his father.

"My son, consider your answers well. A man's life is at stake, but also be aware that vengeance for the taking of another's life, a friend's life, is also very much in our thoughts. Do not give your answers lightly. Speak the truth as you see it. Do you so swear?"

Orlando nodded.

"Say it!" his father rumbled.

"I so swear." Orlando seemed embarrassed at being corrected in front of the old men. Alonzo was embarrassed for him.

"Did you look for a weapon, a sword of any kind?"

"I did. We all did, except Tomas who was guarding him. When we saw the way Grigori was cut about, we

41

went everywhere, looked everywhere, but we couldn't find a sword or any cutting thing, hatchet or any blade. Had I found one, I would have executed him myself."

The Shero Rom frowned. "You searched?"

"We followed the tracks he made – went everywhere he'd been and searched as far as a sword could have been thrown in any direction. There was no sign of him burying anything . . . except the old man," Orlando added as an afterthought.

"What about a horse?"

"There was no horse, although there were signs of horses all around the front door."

"Horses or one horse?" the Shero Rom snapped.

"After all that time none of us could tell. There were a lot of hoof prints, but it could have been one horse ridden round and round, or many."

"What opinion do you form of the young man?"

"Well," Orlando turned to look at the King, "I think he's a blackguard who is putting on a very clever act of being stupid, and he's deliberately lying to lead us away from the truth."

"What do you consider to be the truth of what happened?" the Shero Rom asked.

"I consider him to be a very clever thief and a liar, who killed Grigori in cold blood intent on robbing him. I believe his horse bolted in some way, galloping off with his sword caught in the harness or somewhere. I think he fell and knocked himself senseless and I fear that has in some way sent him a bit mad . . . "

"First things first," interrupted the Romany leader. "Why do you consider him to be a thief?"

"Well," said Orlando, delving deep into his pocket, "I

42

searched him while he was unconscious and he had these in his pocket," and out came his hand clutching a wad of crisp new bank notes.

The King's face went white. He had forgotten the money that Grigori had refused to take. He had casually stuffed a handful of the new notes into his pocket when leaving the Palace. He had no idea how much there was there. The gasp that came from the Council of old men seemed to put the lid on it as far as Alonzo was concerned.

The cold voice of the Shero Rom was like a knife thrust. "Is this your money?"

"Yes . . . er, yes, it is," said the King.

"How much money is there?"

"I don't know."

The Shero Rom's voice was relentless as he said, "You don't know how much is there but you are positive that it *is* your money?"

"Yes, I am positive." The King sensed he was being led into some sort of trap but he couldn't see where it lay. Sweat broke out on his forehead and his top lip.

"How long have you had this money?"

"Er . . . I've always had it . . . er, that is, quite recently . . . I had it . . . I got it . . . it's mine."

The Shero Rom took the money, counted it and turning his back on the King he addressed the Council members:

"There is enough money here to buy three horses and a caravan, and yet moments ago you heard this young man say that he had no horse because HE COULD NOT AFFORD ONE!" The last part he shouted at Alonzo as he turned abruptly to face him.

"I didn't want to rob Grigori," Alonzo stammered. "I bought some honey from him . . . er . . . I offered him money, but he said no one trusted the money." There he noticed all the Council giving affirmative nods to one another. At least they agreed with *something* he said.

"So you killed him? Killed him for some honey?"

"No I *didn't*! I took off this coat and gave it to him in exchange for the honey. He said it was barter. This was my coat and he was wearing it when he was killed – you can see the sword cuts through the material." He ripped the coat off in panic and thrust it into the old man's hands.

The Shero Rom examined the coat. "How do you come to be wearing this coat now?"

"When I buried him I thought I might need the coat as some kind of proof of what happened, and then I was so cold I had to put it on to keep warm." This was all true, the King thought, they couldn't catch him out now.

"You stayed in Grigori's hut. Why did you not light a fire to keep warm?"

"I didn't know how to." The King's voice was a mere whisper.

"Was the tinder box missing?" The puzzled Shero Rom turned to ask Orlando.

"It was all there. The first thing we did was to light a fire," Orlando replied in a disgusted sort of voice. You could see he had difficulty in believing anything that Alonzo said.

The jacket was passed from man to man amongst the Council. Here and there a murmured comment was heard, but mostly they were making up their minds in silence. Eventually it was returned to the Shero Rom who handed it back to Alonzo. For want of something to do in the silence Alonzo put the coat back on over his peasant shirt and stood there uncertain as to what would happen next.

"Do you want to tell us the truth, young man?" The Shero Rom finally asked in a gentle voice, and Orlando turned and he too stared at the young King. Everyone was staring at him. What should he say?

"Is that *your* own coat you are wearing?" The old Romany's voice was still soft, almost friendly in its tone.

"Yes, it's mine," Alonzo said in desperation. The old man slowly turned to face the Council. He stood with his back to Orlando and the King.

"You have heard the evidence and must decide as to guilt or innocence. I find it very strange that an honest man, who says he cannot afford a horse, who wears such an old and poor jacket, has in his pocket enough money, which he claims is his own, to buy five gentleman's suits, or a brace of fine-matched carriage horses. This man claims he never owned a horse. This man claims he never learnt to use a sword and says he knows nothing of making a fire. Where has he grown up, you should ask yourself? In some grand palace perhaps where everything is done for him, where his *fine* clothes are cleaned daily by some *servant*?"

The old men were all laughing now, but not in a nice way. The laughter did not reach their eyes. The King's skin seemed to boil, and in a flash of rage he stepped forward and, grabbing the old man by the shoulder, he pulled him roughly around so that they faced each other.

"Yes!" he shouted. "Yes, in a palace! I'm your . . ."

He never finished the sentence. Orlando's bunched

45

fist caught him on the side of the head and he had the impression of fireworks exploding everywhere. The next thing he knew he was kneeling on all fours with his mouth hanging open as the two guards rushed forward to manhandle him to his feet.

Orlando was rubbing the knuckles of his hand, and as the King was held upright, he said, "Never lay your hands on the Romany Shero Rom again. He is our King."

"No, *I* am your King!" Alonzo shouted. There. It was out now. All movement seemed to stop as if the world was suddenly frozen. Alonzo was aware of the coppery taste of blood in his mouth where he had been hit.

"This is the lie he tried to tell us at the hut," Orlando said quietly to his father.

"Did you tell him of the proclamation?"

Orlando nodded.

Slowly the Shero Rom turned to Alonzo.

"The King died days ago of food poisoning and his body was cremated. What have you to say to that?"

"It's all lies," Alonzo said. He realised he had started in a rush, and tried to calm himself down so that his words would sound like the truth as he told of his foray into the markets, his carefree "game" where he went in disguise to buy some honey for the Royal breakfast. At least I have their attention, he thought as the story unfolded. Then as quickly as it had begun, it was finished. The whole story was out. The wig, the fact that he had recognised Count Tzlenko's bodyguard – everything up to the hearing of the soldiers' discussion after the murder, and his realisation that the old beekeeper had been killed in mistake for himself.

46

He stopped talking.

The silence was absolute. Everyone was just looking at him.

"Don't you see?" cried the King. "He poisoned the whole of the guard so that he should never be accused of the King's murder. Then he said the King had died of food poisoning too! Oh, can't you see it? He then executed the kitchen staff – the only ones who would be able to tell everyone that the King never sat down to that meal. How could he? He was lying exhausted in a beekeeper's hut. Please, you must *believe* me!" He looked from one face to the next.

The Shero Rom turned to his son and asked, "Did you see anything of a wig? It seems to be a very important part of this young man's story."

"There was no sign of any wig!"

Alonzo covered his eyes with one hand and tried to visualise every action of his dreadful burial task. His eyes were screwed shut with the concentration, but try as he might, he could not remember seeing the wig after old Grigori was killed. Surely it would have been in the makeshift grave? Alonzo tried to explain, but the Council was no longer listening. There was no point in saying any more.

The Shero Rom called for silence.

"Young man, you will be returned to your caravan where you will be secured and guarded, and as soon as we have reached a verdict you will be brought back here to know of it. Gentlemen, call me when you have made up your minds." He turned and moved away to his caravan as the two guards tied Alonzo's hands together behind his back and marched him back to where the quiet and solemn Turon waited.

The Romany lad took one look at Alonzo's face and his heart sank.

"My god, Cockroach," he shook his head, "you told them all that King stuff."

*   *   *

Waiting in the caravan was probably the most nerve-racking thing that had ever happened to Alonzo, and when at last, after dark, he was summoned to hear the verdict it was a great relief – any sort of action would have been a relief.

Turon gave him a silent nod as he was led away by the two guards to where the old men had gathered around an open crackling fire. The young King tried to guess the verdict by looking at the men, but it was as if each face had been carefully closed towards him. No man would meet his eyes and that, in itself, filled him with dread.

As soon as he was standing in front of the Council, the Shero Rom said in a low voice, "Let me have your verdicts."

One by one the old men came up and whispered in his ear. The first three men went and stood on the Shero Rom's left hand side, the fourth went and stood on his right.

From then on the young King watched with mounting nerves as each Council member went to one side or the other. There were many more going to the left than to the right, and by the time the whole group had passed on their decision to the Shero Rom there were only three men standing on his right hand side. The old man turned, and with a straight face he said:

"It is the decision of the majority of the Council of Elders that you are guilty of the murder of our friend Grigori. Several did not think you guilty of the killing of our friend but at the same time they could not find it in their hearts to believe any of your story, so they have gone along with the majority. I have my own thoughts, but in this case the death penalty I am afraid is the only one."

5

Alonzo felt as if his limbs had turned to water and, had the guards not been clutching his arms, he would surely have fallen.

"Tomorrow at dusk, I decree that you will meet our best swordsman. Normally you would be unarmed, but I have decided that you shall be given a sword." There was a sudden uproar all around him, but the Shero Rom raised his voice and continued, "If you succeed in disarming him or defeating him in any way short of actually killing him – then you are free to go. Is that clear?"

He had almost to shout the last question as the Council of Elders expressed their disgust.

"That is my decision as Shero Rom," he shouted. "If you do *not* like it, then you have the right to depose me. Until such time as you do depose me, my decision stands. What say you?"

The old men stood grumbling, but making no move to answer. Eventually, the Shero Rom, grim-faced, turned to Alonzo.

"Food will be brought to you, and tomorrow during the day you may make whatever practice you care to make. Then you will meet our master swordsman,

Gascon, and choose your weapon. As I said, if you can defeat him, you are free to go. Do you have anything to say?"

The young King looked up at the stern face of the old Romany leader, and realised nothing he said would make any difference. He shook his head and slowly turned away. The two guards marched him back to the now familiar caravan and up the steps to where Turon was still waiting. No word was needed, no questioning glance. Had he been declared not guilty, he would, of course, have been free to stroll back unaccompanied.

In another part of the camp, Orlando waited impatiently at the open door of a caravan while Gascon, the swordsman, made himself presentable. It wasn't every day his evening meal was interrupted by a summons from the great Shero Rom. Rumour had already raced around the camp like wildfire, and he was aware that he was to execute this stranger on the following day, so what reason could the Shero Rom have for calling him to a special meeting? He'd done this sort of thing twice before and on both occasions he had been sickened by the whole thing . . . but, it was the will of the Council, it was Romany law and he had to accept it or leave the camp forever.

The thing that mystified him was that on both previous occasions one of the Council members had come to his caravan and just told him directly. Why all the mystery this time?

"But what do you do if someone insults you?"

"No one ever has," Alonzo answered truthfully.

51

"No . . . you know what I mean. If you get into a fight over anything . . . what do you do?" Turon waited. "If someone slapped your face or attacked you . . . eh?"

"They wouldn't dare," Alonzo muttered.

"Oh Gottfried Stutz! Don't give me that King stuff again. This is real. This is tomorrow." Turon looked quite angry. "Look, this is serious. Say I was walking past and you attacked me." Turon matched his actions to his words and moved past Alonzo. "Go on, grab me!" he said over his shoulder, "I'll show you – go on!"

Alonzo unwillingly took hold of Turon's shoulders in a half-hearted way and immediately the boy spun him away, at the same time ducking down into a crouch as he turned and coming up with a wicked-looking short bladed knife.

Alonzo gasped, more from the shock of seeing the knife than from being flung back against the wall of the caravan.

"We all carry one," said Turon. "And we all fool around with mock fights, but if anyone seriously insults you, you've got to fight."

There was a long silence as Turon slipped down into a squatting position with his back against the wall. The two of them sat and stared at each other. "What are we going to do with you?" Turon muttered to himself. He slipped the knife back into the turned over top of his leather boot where it sat snug in a little sheath.

Some distance away in the night came the sounds of a fiddle . . . Just a few scraped notes at first, then the tuning up of a string, a couple of plucked notes, like drops of water, and then the beginning of a plaintive tune. Then someone joined in on a set of pipes.

"Grigori." Turon said.

"What?"

"It's a lament for our old friend."

And for me, thought Alonzo. The music filled him with an unutterable sadness and he saw again the horsemen bunched in the distance, the flashing swords, and in a sudden about face the scene had moved in his mind to the Palace and his last fumbling attempts at sword practice with his sword master. He saw quite clearly the look of disdain on the teacher's face as he half-heartedly attempted to learn the moves. If only he had tried harder. *If only* – there they were again – useless words.

This was real now. What was he going to do tomorrow? He would die. There was no way he could defend himself.

"Come on, Cockroach."

This time it wasn't a cheap insult. It felt like the nicest, friendliest thing anyone had ever said to him in his whole life.

Turon had moved across and was patting him on the shoulders with both hands and suddenly it was too much for the young King.

Turon was amazed and a bit taken aback to find himself clutching a sobbing, shuddering, terrified young man five years older than himself, and realising that he was acting the role of a father comforting a little boy. He pulled a "good heavens, I hope nobody I know ever sees me doing something like this" sort of expression to the empty wall of the caravan, and tried to get into a less awkward position.

In the long run, the music helped. It became a sort of reassuring familiar background, and the exhaustion of the Romany trial and all that had gone before, worked together with the lament to slide Alonzo downwards into merciful sleep.

Turon busied himself arranging what bedding he could find to make the sleeping King as comfortable as he could. As he crouched there, looking at the young face, he had the strange feeling that he was now responsible for this other human being. He had unwittingly taken on the task of looking after him, and he felt that their future . . . "Future?" he muttered to himself, would there be any future for the young man after tomorrow? Turon stopped thinking and stared at the wall. It seemed to dissolve before his intense gaze and he felt himself moving quite rapidly in some ghostly way across and above the campsite, seeing the funeral pyre of dear old Grigori way below him, the sad, sweet music lifting him up and on to some far distant time in which he and Alonzo were forever linked.

Alonzo was ravenously hungry when Turon shook him awake in the morning. It was just after first light and the smell of food was delicious. He tucked in with a will, devouring everything before him. The cottage cheese rolled up in a little square of muslin cloth was deliciously sharp and tart and the slices of bread with what he supposed was sheep's fat were just salty enough. The coffee, Turon explained, was made from acorns roasted over an open fire and then ground up. It *was* slightly bitter and not what he was used to, but some honey added from the decorated pottery bowl and stirred in with the wooden honey spoon, made it very palatable. Something about the resigned look on Turon's face, the eyebrows slightly raised as if to say, "Ah well . . . " finally got through to Alonzo.

"Have you eaten?" he said.

"Well, I wasn't hungry anyway," Turon replied, shuffling his feet. "You obviously could have wolfed down that much again. Don't worry. You'll need it."

Turon's remark brought the day's forthcoming ordeal forward in Alonzo's mind.

"Don't worry," said Turon. "Do you want to work out some tactics? I've seen Gascon fight many times and

55

I gather the Shero Rom has allowed you time for sword practice. I can help you," he rattled on, ignoring Alonzo's look of mounting despair, mixed with panic. "He's very good, but he always fights the same way and if we can upset his caravan a bit for him . . . you might . . ."

"It's no good," said Alonzo, in a small voice. "I never learnt how to swordfight." His food already felt curdled and leaden in his stomach. A few short hours and he'd be dead. What use to try and learn how to handle a sword now?

"Come on, Cockroach," Turon urged. "Listen, Gascon's best with the rapier," he continued, "so we'll keep away from those – I've got a couple of wooden practice swords here for us."

Alonzo picked one up and examined it with remarkable lack of enthusiasm.

"Come on. I'm Gascon. Now . . . he always starts with a move like this which is designed to trick you into moving over to your left to parry, but don't do it. Be ready to go the other way." Turon accompanied the words with a rapid series of sword flourishes to Alonzo's left, ending up with a round-house slash to Alonzo's neck from the other side. The blow connected with a sickening thud. Alonzo dropped the sword with a yelp and fell to his knees clutching both hands to his neck, his forehead on the dewy grass.

"Gottfried Stutz, Cockroach!" Turon was down on his hands and knees shouting point blank at the King. "Didn't you hear me? I told you everything I was going to do, I *told* you . . . I could have killed you! What's the matter with you? Cockroach? . . . Answer me!"

"It's no good," Alonzo gasped painfully, his forehead still thrust hard against the grass. "Forget about trying to help me. Go away – leave me to die. Leave me alone." The pain in his neck and shoulder was excruciating.

"What do you want to do?"

"Nothing . . . just help me back inside." Alonzo's voice was a barely audible mumble.

In the caravan Turon was busy trying to rub some life back into the bruised neck muscle. Alonzo winced at every move. Finally he flung his arms up and knocked the young Romany's hand away. "Leave it," he said petulantly. "Get a razor and shave me. I'm not going to my death looking like this."

"Don't order me around, Cockroach. I'll be your friend, but I'm damned if I'll be your slave."

There was a long pause while the two eyed each other, then Turon added, "I haven't started shaving yet, so I don't own a razor, and anyway, Orlando's forbidden you to have such a thing, in case you do away with yourself."

"Hah!" a disgusted grunt from the young King, and the silence descended again.

After a long time in which Turon tried to find something to do, Alonzo said "Sorry" very quietly. A look passed between them and Turon did a little flick upwards of his eyebrows just to acknowledge the apology.

There was one rat-tat-tat of banging on the door when the guards came with an offer of more food, but that was rejected and all too soon came the dreaded moment. There was Orlando to conduct the condemned man to the middle of camp. As they approached, it seemed that every man and woman and child was gathered for the spectacle. *Well, of course, they probably are*, Alonzo thought as he made a sort of tuneless whistle by sucking air in between his teeth, just to keep his spirits up. The crowd parted to let him through.

There was a big circle cleared in the middle, and in the firelight Alonzo couldn't see one friendly face as he was steered forward by Orlando and the guards to where the Shero Rom stood flanked by his Council.

In the hush, the old man's voice was like the rumble of some bass viol.

"Are you ready, young man?"

Alonzo nodded. He couldn't trust his voice.

"It is your privilege to choose your weapon." The Shero Rom turned. "Gascon!" he called, and out of the crowd stepped a wiry-looking man clutching six assorted weapons.

"Rapier, broad sword or sabre?" he asked, with absolutely no emotion in his voice.

Alonzo had an immediate picture of one of his valets offering up different garments while dressing him in the Palace: "Red, turquoise, or green silk, your Majesty?" he had said, in the same bored voice.

He became aware that everyone was staring at him with questioning faces, eyebrows raised. They needed an answer. Alonzo sucked in a deep breath and said, "Rapier."

There was a buzz of voices around the circle, and loud and clear from behind, he heard Turon's anguished cry, "*No*, Cockroach!"

Somebody laughed at the supposed insult and it was

58

done. A Romany helper was taking the other four weapons away and Gascon was presenting the two rapiers, handles forward, towards the young King. The next few moments seemed to go into a dream. Everything slowed down. Alonzo saw himself grasp one of the weapons and it took forever to slide towards him over Gascon's forearm where it rested.

Then someone, he presumed it was the Shero Rom, was giving instructions to the pair of them.

He heard nothing. It was as if all his senses had switched off.

"On guard!" He heard that, but it was slowed down to a low rumble, all the urgency gone out of it.

"Fight!"

He was aware of Gascon, his left arm raised and bent downwards at the wrist, lunging in slow motion at him with the other arm. There was nothing he could do. The blade went through the material of his shirt and deep into his shoulder and suddenly everything jolted back into real time, real sound. A great yell went up from the crowd and Alonzo looked in stunned amazement as the rapier tip slid back out of his flesh. He felt no pain at all, he supposed that would come later, but the sight of the blood . . . his blood, filled him with a sudden frenzy of anger.

"Attack the King would you?" he yelled and lunged forward with a flurry of as many attacking moves as he could remember from those far-off disastrous lessons.

It was no use. Gascon, master swordsman, contemptuously avoided the tip of his blade and in three slashing moves at the end of Alonzo's sequence of strokes, he neatly removed almost the whole of the front of

Alonzo's shirt and left a deep gash on his chest right above the heart.

The sound from the crowd was a continuous roar now. It was like some huge animal, sensing and wanting the kill.

Gascon easily evaded Alonzo's rapier blade. In fact, with a sort of twirling spiral movement, he casually manoeuvred the King's sword until it was facing completely in the wrong direction and then, with a contemptuous backwards and forwards move, he skewered the muscle at the top of Alonzo's sword arm.

"ENOUGH!" The Shero Rom's voice was loud when he wanted it to be. The yelling of the crowd died to a mutter as Gascon turned on his heel and walked towards the edge of the circle.

The crowd parted in disbelief and he stalked through the narrow path made for him with never a glance to either side. As he left, the crowd turned its attention back to the centre of the ring.

The Shero Rom smoothed his white moustache with two nervous sweeps of his hand, cleared his throat, and said, "I arranged it all with Gascon last night." The silence was absolute. Every eye was on him as he continued. "He was to wound the prisoner as painfully as he could. If the young man had been spurred to action and shown any skill with the sword I would have known his words of defence were lies and would have signalled Gascon to finish it. As you saw, he showed as much skill as a five-year-old child, and remember . . . he knew he was fighting for his life!" The old man turned to where Alonzo stood, the blood running from his arms and chest. "You are free to go."

He turned on his heel and walked away, his head held high as members of the Council of old men rushed to him, voices raised. Hands tugged at his sleeves, everyone was suddenly shouting, but still the old man stalked forward with such dignity that a path miraculously appeared before him and people in front of him felt forced to drop their eyes from his fierce gaze.

Orlando and the guards were joined by Turon and together, almost unnoticed, they shepherded the stumbling young King back to the caravan. This time the guards were there to *protect* him.

"You're a very lucky man," Orlando said. "My father half-believed you. As he said, you're free to go, but what he didn't say is, you're not free to stay. Nobody wants you here. They still think you killed the old man. I, myself . . . I don't know what to make of you." He turned to Turon. "See to his wounds." And almost as an afterthought, "You'd better make sure you lock this door after us. Once you're healed up, you're on your own!"

This last statement was directed at Alonzo and the son of the Shero Rom flung open the door and pushed his way through the grumbling crowd that had now surrounded the caravan. The two guards followed him out, and quickly Turon closed and locked the door. Taking a big breath, he turned and looked at his exhausted friend.

"I never thought I'd see you alive again, Cockroach. I died a thousand deaths out there watching you." He shook his head and turned to the fireplace, busying himself with the simple problem of heating up some water to wash the King's wounds.

The next few days were a hotchpotch of pain, sleeping and eating for Alonzo. His chest wound wasn't so bad. Turon had cooked up some Romany poultice of leaves and the bark of various trees and the crushed up roots of some plant or other, and this was smeared onto clean linen and tied on to his chest and arms. The wounds had first been washed with hot, stinging, salty water. Alonzo had had no experience of this side of life, and Turon's insistence on scrubbing away all the dried blood and every scrap of possible dirt out of the open cut had seemed both painful *and* unnecessary. The King was very lethargic in the aftermath of the tension and exhaustion of the fight, however, and just couldn't be bothered to argue. So he had to put up with the stinging, put up with all the fussing just to have it finished.

The progress was slow but eventually came the day when the bandages came off for good.

"Well, you're on your own now, Konstantin," Turon said.

"My name is Alonzo. How many times must I tell you?"

"I feel awkward calling you that," said Turon, "and it always reminds everybody of that cock-and-bull story you told. That's embarrassing."

"What must I do to prove it to you?" Alonzo asked, turning away in despair.

"If you could find the ginger wig I'd believe you."

The King spun round to face the boy. "Who told *you* about the wig?"

"I overheard Orlando laughing to some of his cronies about it," Turon replied. "They were all a bit stupid on wine, and you'd never believe it but Orlando turns into quite a lovable, laughing character when he's drunk."

As Turon had been speaking the King was reliving in his mind the gruesome business of the burial. Turon's words seemed to recede into the distance and eventually into silence. The King was not hearing him at all. He was pin-pointing in his mind the moment he had decided to take the jacket from the old beekeeper's body. It must have been during the awkward dragging off of the coat that the wig had been dislodged. He had been exhausted and it was fully dark by that time. He had scraped as much earth as he could back over the body. The wig *must* still be there!

His eyes slowly refocused and he became aware of the silence and of Turon staring at him.

"What happens now?" he asked.

"What happens where?" Turon replied.

"Here, now . . . what happens about me?" said the King, slightly petulantly.

"Don't get up on your high horse, Cockroach. I told you I'm not your servant." Turon raised his eyebrows in a semi-comic face, which took all the sting out of the words. The King smiled.

"Sorry," he said, "I just need to know what I'm supposed to do."

"Well, the truth of the matter is, nobody wants anything to do with you. The sooner you're away from here the happier everyone will be." Turon paused. "Every time anyone sees me bringing food or medicine to the caravan, that nasty crowd feeling flares up again. People are blaming the Shero Rom, though they won't say anything . . . so *he* wants you gone as well. As soon

63

as you're fit you've got to leave. That means today."

"But where will I go?"

Turon shrugged.

"What will I eat?"

Once again came the "I don't know" look on Turon's face, the raised eyebrows, the shrug.

They looked at each other in silence and Alonzo realised how much he had come to rely on this lad. "Could you guide me back to Grigori's hut? I could live on honey and what I could gather in the forest, and if we can find that wig, then maybe people will believe me."

"I'm not allowed to," said Turon. "I'm supposed to escort you out of the camp and that's the end of it." The King stared at him for such a long time that Turon began to feel uncomfortable. "Could you ride on a horse behind me?" he said at last.

Alonzo said "Yes" in such an eager voice it was like an untrained puppy who gets a little bit of kindness and then jumps all over you.

"I was just asking." Turon turned away. A second later he spun round. "Look . . . don't start licking my boots just because I'm trying to think of a way to help you. You're five years *older* than me, for God's sake. I don't *want* you being so pathetically grateful."

Alonzo looked away. "It's not easy to think like this. Everyone's always done everything for me. I've never had to beg for anything before."

"So don't start now!"

The King had never been so cold. His whole body was shuddering as he waited outside the Romany camp. Some noise in the night alerted him, and he turned.

In the distance he saw a ghostly patch of lighter colour and realised, as it came closer, that it was a big old carthorse. Then he could see Turon. The boy was covered in a dark blanket that seemed to drape almost to the ground as he walked. He had hold of the harness with one hand and the other was resting lightly on the horse's nose. As they drew level with the big tree that surged up all bent and gnarled from the edge of Alonzo's hiding place, Turon hissed, "Konstan?"

"Here," he whispered in reply, and Turon quickly covered the horse's nostrils as it snorted and drew back in alarm.

"You all right?" Turon whispered back.

"Cold!" shuddered Alonzo.

"Can't help that for the moment. We've got to get away from here." Alonzo was amazed to see the boy wrap his arms around the horse's head and kiss the horse on the nose. He was a bit embarrassed, he realised, by this obvious show of affection, but at the same time it seemed to forge them into a team of three conspirators, rather than two conspirators and a horse. He felt good.

"Let him smell your hand," Turon said.

The King uncoiled his stiff limbs from the spot where he had hidden in the bracken and stretched out his hand.

The horse jerked back his head and then turned it to one side, the whites of his eyes seeming to glow huge in the night.

"Don't you know *anything* about horses?" Turon's whisper had a bite to it. "Don't hold your hand in front of him where he can't see it. A horse's eyes are on the side. Gottfried Stutz!" He heaved a big sigh.

Alonzo swallowed the angry answer he was going to give and let the horse see his offered hand – then gently patted him on the forehead. The horse was still a bit jumpy.

"Breathe down his nose," Turon whispered.

"What?"

"Sssh . . . look . . . just do as I say. Come towards him gently where he can see what you're doing, then breathe out of your nose so the air goes into his nose.

Horses do it as a friendly gesture. Come on!" Turon's whisper was getting an edge of desperation to it.

Feeling very silly, Alonzo did as he was told, breathing awkwardly with his nose almost touching the horse's nose. To his amazement, the horse did exactly the same in return and the warm horsey smell of his breath was very comforting.

"Petronstanz is his name. Petro we call him. He's one of the family. Right . . . we've got to move." Turon grabbed the horse's mane, did two little running steps and jumped and turned all in one, his right leg flinging up and over the horse's back. He landed lightly in a sitting position and looked down at Alonzo.

"Your arm, Konstantin, not your hand, it would tear open your wound again. Grip my shoulder and put your elbow in my hand – now jump!"

They made three attempts in the dark before Alonzo could scramble up into a sitting position behind his friend. His left shoulder was screaming with pain but he clenched his jaw, eyes jammed shut and held his breath until the fierce spasm had passed. "I'm growing up," he thought, imagining the tantrum such pain would have brought only half a year ago. His pent up breath came shuddering out, and straight away the shivering started again.

"Throw the blanket over you," whispered Turon. It was a big blanket Turon was wearing, his head thrust through an embroidered hole in the centre, and Alonzo was soon snuggled up in the dark, underneath it, getting some warmth from Turon's back.

At a signal from Turon's knees the horse moved quietly off, and when they were well away from the

Romany camp the gentle walk became a distance-eating jog trot. Alonzo didn't notice. With his arms clutched around Turon's waist he was fast asleep in the darkness.

"We're back at the Palace, your Majesty." Turon's laughing voice was quite relaxed and loud. Alonzo woke up with a start and struggled out from under the blanket. They were on the dirt road, in front of the old beekeeper's hut. Memories came flooding back, pictures of those nightmare days. The King sat staring ahead into the gloom until eventually Turon's voice jolted him out of his dream.

"Come on, Cockroach, I've got to get back before dawn or they'll skin me alive. I wasn't supposed to help you, you know, just escort you out of the camp and make sure you left."

He hooked one leg over and slid effortlessly down to the ground. "Mind your arms," he said as he helped Alonzo down. "Now, were you *really* serious about making a fire?"

"What do you mean?"

"You really and truly and honestly don't know how to use a tinder box?"

"I've never even seen one to my knowledge," said Alonzo.

Turon shook his head and made disbelieving noises, sort of tut-tutting with his tongue. "Right, I'll show you once and then you're on your own. I've *got* to go." He crouched down, taking a small tin box from his pocket as he did so, and said, "Get down here and watch."

Alonzo crouched down and peered through the

gloom. "This is tinder – any sort of rotted wood or fine grass, all dried and teased out with your fingernails. You need some dry sticks – very thin, but I haven't time now – just so you know. You take these two bits of stone . . ." He sharply banged them together and a spark briefly lit up the darkness. "See?"

Alonzo nodded. It was so simple he couldn't believe it.

"You've got to direct that spark down onto the tinder and blow on it, like this." In a very short space of time, the tinder glowed and flared briefly into flame. "That's when you need the sticks and then, when those are burning you put on the firewood. Right – I've got to go now."

As they stood up, he closed the tinder box and gave it to Alonzo. "I'll get back when I can, my friend." He vaulted up onto the horse, the huge blanket flapping about him.

My friend. The words burnt in Alonzo's brain. No one had *ever* said that to him before.

"I nearly forgot." Turon unhooked the old cooking pot from the harness and passed it down. "You remember old Grigori's pot? Right – and his knife as well." He pulled the well-worn knife out from where it had been jammed down behind his belt and passed it, handle forward, to the King.

"Got to go . . . good luck!" And at a knee signal, old Petro lumbered off into the darkness.

It was all so quick. One minute they were there, the next, he was waving goodbye and they were out of sight, just the clop-clop of the hooves carried back on the night air, fainter and fainter.

Alonzo slowly turned, a great sense of loneliness

69

6

It was a month of amazing learning, or so it seemed to Alonzo, tremendous growth in every direction, growth in his knowledge, in his ability to do all sorts of things he'd never dreamed of doing, and most of all, in his self-confidence. Just being able to build his own fire and get it to light was like the greatest present he'd ever had in his life. He was feeding himself. At first it was very basic food, but he wasn't starving. The cooking pot was forever on the go and he had experimented with anything that he thought might be edible. He'd had some disastrous results but that just meant an empty stomach until the next day when he could go foraging again.

He had trimmed down, no longer the podgy spoilt brat that he recognised from his previous memory of himself, but a slimmer, straighter, more confident man. He stopped in mid-thought . . . yes . . . *man*.

He smiled as he remembered Turon's face when he had come back that first time. He had obviously come wondering if Alonzo was still alive. Well . . . he had been very much alive, and the first thing he had done was to show the Romany boy the mud-covered ginger wig. He had found it the day after that midnight horse ride. It was, as he had thought it must be, all

71

covered in earth in the makeshift grave he had dug for Grigori, all that time ago.

He would never forget the look on Turon's face as he realised what the existence of that wig must mean, that all Alonzo's "King stuff" was true. He had stood there, open-mouthed, not sure how to address this bearded young man, and Alonzo had stepped forward, right hand outstretched, to take all the awkwardness out of the situation.

"How shall we remain?" he said, smiling at the Romany lad. "Friends, I hope."

Turon grasped his hand, not knowing what to say, then let go of the hand and gave Alonzo a huge hug, hiding his embarrassment in laughter.

"What do I call you?" he finally said.

Alonzo pulled back from the embrace and holding Turon at arm's length, one hand on each shoulder, he said, "You can call me whatever you want to call me. You are the first friend I've ever had in my whole life." He paused, his eyes locked with Turon's eyes, and then continued, "I'll never forget that . . . call me Konstantin." They both laughed, the tension suddenly gone. "I've rather got used to it." He carried on, "Come and have something to eat."

They went into the hut and to Turon's amazement shared vegetable stew followed by some honey from a broken clay pot that was wedged on its side between the old table and the wall.

"How did you get the honey?" Turon asked. "Surely we took all the honey Grigori had left here."

"You did," the King replied. "I got some more. I was fascinated by everything Grigori told me about the bees.

72

I knew absolutely nothing and he seemed to know everything . . . so, he just told me all he could think of. He showed me his gloves and the hat with the net cover to keep the bees out, and he explained about his little tin and leather smoke box. So . . . you'd shown me how to make a fire and I smoked them a bit, lifted the roof off one of the hives, and took some honeycomb out . . . didn't get stung at all. Grigori had told me they only attack if they feel you're scared, so . . . I thought about how nice the honey would taste. I was *dying* for something sweet by then."

"You amaze me, Konstantin," Turon said. "You've grown up. You were such a child."

"Child or no child, I'm really craving some meat of some sort. You haven't got any sausage or bacon or . . ."

"I've got a bit of goat's cheese you can have, " Turon replied, "and meat's easy. All you have to do is catch a hedgehog."

"A hedgehog?" Alonzo's stomach turned over. "Ugh!" He couldn't stop the feeling of revulsion.

"Stop all that King stuff," Turon started, and then stopped in embarrassment. "Er . . . what I meant was . . ."

Alonzo shook his head in a friendly way. "You don't have to guard your tongue with me, my friend. What were you going to say?"

"I was going to say there's no way you can catch a bit of rare roast beef with hollandaise sauce or snare a chunk of pork or venison, but I can show you how to catch a porcupine. They make quite a noise at night when they're feeding. You've just got to sneak up and surprise them and they roll into a ball."

"What about all the spikes?"

"What *we* do is pack the spikes full of clay – easy. You make them into a big ball of clay and then build a fire round them . . ."

He stopped and heaved a sigh – "Look, don't go pulling those faces at me – you turn into a child again – you must know if you want to eat meat, something's got to die, all right? I'm just explaining what *we* do. So, you cook it until the clay's all dried out and baked really hard, then you roll it out of the fire and wait for it to cool a bit. Then you bash the clay and all the skin and the spikes come away attached to the clay and it's delicious. Very rich – pity you don' t have some bread to mop up the fat. A hedgehog is too rich to eat all at once – so it could last you a few days, easily."

"What about the fleas?"

Turon burst out laughing. "If they haven't got the sense to desert a sizzling hedgehog, then you've just got to make sure you bake the clay really hard, then you take the clay into one of the foundries in the capital and they'll cast some beautiful little fleas for you – in bronze – life size!" Turon was doubled over laughing, slapping his knees and eventually Alonzo joined in laughing. It was a ridiculous picture.

"Listen," Turon continued, "if I bring you back a few pots, do you think you could fill them with honey? Then I could take it to the Shero Rom together with the wig and they may let you come back. What do you think?"

"Well, the wig should prove I was telling the truth," Alonzo started.

"They'll never believe the King stuff," Turon cut in, "that's too much. But that wig together with the possibility of more honey, could change their minds."

The wig had indeed made the difference – it wasn't the sort of thing you could manufacture while living alone in a peasant's hut. Turon had asked to see the Shero Rom and Orlando had come to summon him that evening. Orlando had stayed as a sort of bodyguard for his father during the whole of the meeting.

To Turon's surprise, it had been a very informal affair. After the first formal greeting the Shero Rom had poured three small glasses of fiery home-made cherry brandy, which they'd all tossed down, Turon coughing most of his up his nose it seemed as the spirit bit at his throat. Then they sat around the table while Turon confessed to his friendship with Alonzo, his secret meetings back at Grigori's hut, and the fact that Alonzo was able to provide them with honey as Grigori had done.

Here Turon had brought out a jar of honey from the sack and they broke the wax seal and sampled it with some surprise and pleasure. The bombshell had come when he had produced the wig.

Both the Shero Rom and his son had stood up, Orlando a little more slowly than his father.

"I told you I believed the boy," the old man said. "What possible reason could he have for making up such a far-fetched story?"

Turon had been formally thanked and sent on his way and the next day, after a meeting of the Council, a sullen-faced Orlando had to tell Turon that his friend could return on one condition. He should not be a burden on the Romany community. Turon was to be responsible for seeing that Alonzo paid his way some-how. A bit of honey now and again was a bonus, but

. . . and it was left in the air as to what useful employment Turon could find for his friend. So it was arranged that Alonzo came back to the camp.

The next few weeks seemed to run together as a hotchpotch of different pictures in Alonzo's mind. He was half-accepted by most of the younger Romanies, but treated with suspicion and sometimes outright hostility by the old-timers.

The Shero Rom's decision was final however, and there was no question of Alonzo being driven out of the camp, it was just that everywhere he turned he felt he had to prove himself.

He was helped all along the line by Turon's friendship of course, but he knew that he had to win respect by the sort of person he himself was and not by the sort of friends he had.

That first night he tried to sleep, cold and rough on some straw under Turon's family caravan with a hastily built windbreak on three sides, and an extra coat and Turon's blanket cloak covering him.

It was a miserable night and he spent the next day trying to make something which was a little more proof against the wind. It was a nice surprise to find that two Romany twins, more adventurous than the other children, came to help him. At first, he suspected, they were so surprised to find an adult who knew so little about anything that they thought he must be a bit funny in the head. He caught them, out of the corner of his eye, making the universal "mad" sign to one another, spinning the index finger around alongside the temple indicating that his brain must be going "loopy".

He was so grateful for any help however, and they

were so thrilled to find an adult who didn't chase them away that they rapidly became a team. The twins appointed themselves foremen, ordering the other little ones to the river to get willow twigs and mud, explaining the best way to make a " willow and daub" wall, as they called it.

Alonzo slowly discovered that he had a hidden talent for amusing these young helpers. He made everything into a game, and by pretending to be even more stupid than he felt he was, he found that the children, in mock disgust at his supposed lack of knowledge would make a pantomime of showing him, in minute detail, how to do all the things which, to them, were everyday and obvious. Alonzo was learning everything the way a child naturally learns, one simple step at a time.

There was one thing that happened, quite unexpectedly in that first day, that endeared him instantly to all the children. It happened quite simply when one of the camp dogs barked, away in the distance. When he had been growing up in the Palace, his favourite game, which had driven all his tutors one by one into a suppressed fury, had been to "bark" back at the Palace lapdogs and if possible to start up a fight between them in this way. He had been able to imitate all sorts of different barks and whines and pantings so well that he could completely confuse any dog he ever met.

So here he suddenly found himself the centre of attention from all the children as he "barked" back at the dog. His "barking" was so realistic that he soon had every dog in camp barking and yelping their challenges as they came stalking, stiff legged, hackles all standing on end to attack this unknown new "dog" in camp. The children were open-mouthed in admiration and then were running in every direction giggling and laughing, and from that moment on, Alonzo was quite literally "King of the Kids". Everywhere he went he had an entourage of youngsters following him, waiting for him to do the next "crazy" thing.

When Turon came back from his work at the pottery he was amazed to find that Alonzo was now the proud owner of a sleeping shelter. It was small, constructed on a slight slope so that any heavy rain would run away and its walls, made of woven willow branches and covered inside and out with mud mixed with grass, were wind-proof from three directions.

"Have you thought about food, Konstan?" Turon asked, after his initial surprise had passed.

"Not really," the King sighed. "My stomach is rumbling so much I can't think."

"Can you manage on honey for tonight? I can show you how to set snares later and maybe we can catch a hedgehog. We're not allowed to share food with you unless you do something useful, Orlando says. I'm sorry."

"I knew that before I came back," said the King, "so don't worry about me. I'll manage with some honey and the potatoes I brought back from Grigori's. I thought I'd go out early in the morning and look for mushrooms, but I must say some meat would be a great luxury."

"You'll have to be up early to beat the children. That's their job, mushroom collecting. Did you bring any salt back with you?" Turon asked. Alonzo shook his head.

"Huh! You'll find everything very tasteless without it. I'll see if my mother will let you have some."

Alonzo went to bed fairly hungry that night, but at least he was warm. He had built a small fire in the centre of his sleeping area, mainly to speed up the drying of the mud daub on the walls, but it had the effect of heating up the earth a little so that when he moved the ashes and the coals out to make room for his straw bedding there was quite a cosy warm glow from beneath him.

He re-kindled a little fire a few feet away and went to sleep very quickly, snug under Turon's old coat and blanket.

The following days seemed to be taken up with a constant battle to find enough to eat, brightened only by his meetings with the camp children. No matter how he felt it was expected that he would do something crazy or make some silly sounds to amuse them. So quite simply, he did. It always cheered him up.

They followed him to the pottery when he first started working there, but Silvander, the potter, soon sent them on their way. He was a stern-faced man who stood no nonsense and it had taken a lot of talking from Turon to get his friend a trial job "pugging".

This "pugging" was really boring work, and in the normal run of events, Turon would have done it. It meant that you took the wet clay from the barrow in manageable chunks and threw it down over and over again onto a big plank of wood. Each time you picked up the clay some of the moisture had soaked into the wood and as it got less sloppy, you had to throw it down harder. You had to pull out any bits of sticks or stones, grass or leaves that were dug up with the clay and eventually when the clay was of the right consistency throughout, and just right for modelling or turning on the potter's wheel, it went into a shallow wooden bowl with a wet cloth thrown over the top to stop it drying out.

Alonzo had thought it was a bit childish to take such a small handful of clay so he grabbed as much as he could comfortably hold in two hands and started to slosh it down onto the dry timber. The more he worked the more his back ached. The old stab wounds in his shoulders from his abortive swordfight were playing up very badly every time he raised the clay above head height and in a very short time he forgot his manly pride and halved the size of the ball of clay. As he dropped one half back on the barrow he caught Turon smiling at him in a mischievous way and straight away he blushed furiously.

But the King had changed. He was suddenly able to stand back from himself, as it were, and see the humour of it . . . him trying to be a big man and take twice the load that Turon could manage, and then being caught out.

He stood there and laughed at himself and Turon joined him in the infectious laughter. He started again, and quite rapidly got into a rhythm of working. Very soon he had the wooden bowl filled with "pugged" lumps of clay in manageable sizes.

"What do I do now?" he asked.

The old man came across and looked into the bowl. "Finished already?" He frowned as he picked up one of the lumps and pulled it apart. "You've got to do those all again," he said. "Put a bit more effort into it at the end, and keep breaking up the lumps to see how it's going.

See here . . . there's a small pocket of air like a bubble, trapped in the clay, a bit of stick there too. It's no good half doing the job. I make a bowl with a bubble in the clay and when I fire it, that air bubble expands with the heat and bang! The whole bowl has blown into pieces and probably spoilt half the other things in the firing as well. Do them properly." And he turned and went back to his wheel.

Alonzo took a huge breath and began again. By the time he had finished his task, Turon had two long wooden boards stacked with decorated bowls. Alonzo crouched down to take a short rest, and watched in admiration as his friend scooped the tiny marks out of the wet clay bowls. The repeat pattern went round the top of the outside of the bowl and, miraculously, it seemed, met up exactly with the beginning mark as the bowl was turned full circle. "I could never do that," he thought. "I'd go mad with boredom doing the same thing over and over again." He looked at all the bowls drying on their wooden planks, stacked up the sides of the walls, and they all seemed to be identical in every respect.

"Why don't you do some different? Hm? Turon?"

"What?" The boy was engrossed in his work and had not heard at all.

"I said, why don't you do the pattern different on some of them?" Alonzo genuinely wanted to know.

"I'm no artist," Turon answered. "I just do the pattern. This is our pattern, for this sort of bowl. We've always done it. I started off doing it this way, and it was a long time before I got it right. I'm not going to go experimenting with something new now, am I?"

"Why not?"

"Oh death and set fire to it, now look what you've made me do!" Turon held up the bowl. "The stinking pattern doesn't meet. Look, don't start talking to me while I'm working!"

He was going to throw the pot away as a failure but Alonzo managed to stop his arm. "Don't break it," he said. "That's rather nice, the way that doesn't meet." He took the pot. "If you continued that around a second time . . . here, give me the tool and I'll show you."

Turon jerked his arm away in a huff. "And no one will buy it because it isn't what they've ever bought before. Look, make your own tool if you want to – I've got work to do."

Alonzo, realising he was not wanted at this point, went wandering around the cluttered pottery building. It looked a real mess. There was dried clay and dust over everything. Eventually he found a piece of sharpened stick and an old bit of wire which he wound around the blunt end to make a curved cutting edge for the clay. Using this he completed the spoiled pattern, as he had imagined it. It was, in fact, a mess; the overlapping pattern actually ruined the effect of Turon's original simple design. There didn't seem to be anything more for him to do, so he took a chunk of the pugged clay and found himself making every child's idea of a little man – a head, two arms outstretched from a round-shaped body, and two stumpy legs. He made the head bigger and immediately the whole thing fell over, so he thickened the ends of the legs so that they became a wider base that the whole body could stand on. It looked good. He was really enjoying himself now. The flat thin slab of clay seemed to become Silvander's leather apron without him consciously planning it at all. The apron was too big by far and reached right to the base of the figure, but this gave it a nice comic effect and he found himself smiling as he made two toes of shoes to peep out from underneath.

Alonzo chuckled quietly to himself as he modelled two huge ears and stuck them on to the sides of the head. When he had modelled the whole face, big nose, beard and huge eyebrows with eyes totally disappearing underneath them, he couldn't stop himself from laughing out loud. He was using the sharp end of a wooden stick to put the smile lines in the sides of the eyes when he became aware of the silence from Silvander and Turon. He turned around and the look on Silvander's face and the nervous look from Turon strangled the chuckles in the base of his throat.

Only Silvander's eyes were moving under his frowning brow. They kept darting up to Alonzo's face and down again to the clay figure. Alonzo's relaxed good-feeling evaporated.

"What in the name of all that's holy do you think you're doing?" Silvander's voice cracked out. "Give me that!" and he snatched up the caricature and squelched it back into a shapeless mass of clay. "If you've got nothing to do, weigh up some clay blanks. You're not here to enjoy yourself, you're here because the boy begged me to give you a try-out. Make yourself useful."

He flung the lump of clay into the corner, turned on his heel and strode back to his potter's bench.

Alonzo looked across at the two toes peeping out from under the apron bottom, the only part of his figurine that was recognisable, and felt a deep sadness. He looked up at Turon. The two friends stood in silence.

Eventually Turon showed him how to use the scales to weigh the exact amount of clay needed to make all the pots the same size.

"How boring," he thought as he pinched off little bits of clay to make the exact weight to tip the balance. "How can they do this over and over again – it must drive them mad!"

At the end of the day's work, the King felt as if he had wasted a day. Silvander left without a word and afterwards, when Turon had finished his pots and was closing up the shed for the night, there seemed no way to start a conversation. Eventually they walked back in an uneasy, but companionable silence. When they got back to the camp, Alonzo's heart leapt into his throat.

He couldn't believe his eyes. In his absence, the children had made a proper thatched roof for his sleeping shelter.

The next day Alonzo didn't know where he stood. Turon couldn't advise him, so the two friends set off tentatively for the pottery. When they got there Silvander was already at work and had made five new pots. He watched them come in out of the corner of his eye and as soon as Turon had started decorating the first of his pots for the day, Silvander stopped what he was doing, climbed off his stool which was attached to the foot-driven potter's wheel, and walked over to where Alonzo stood uneasily.

"I want a talk with you," he said quietly as he strode past him.

"*With you?*" thought Alonzo as he followed the big man outside. That sounded quite friendly and not at all snappy and annoyed – different to yesterday.

As soon as they were out of earshot of the pottery hut, Silvander stopped and turned. "You know, I was very annoyed with you yesterday."

It was a statement, not a question. The young King nodded.

"I destroyed your work because of it and I should not have done that."

It was as close to an apology as Silvander could get and still maintain his dignity in front of the young man.

"Do you know why I destroyed it?"

What does he want me to say? thought Alonzo. "Er . . ." he said out loud, "I suppose because I was not doing my work properly."

"No. I was telling my daughter about it last night and I suddenly realised how much I had admired your work."

He paused, looked at the young King's open-mouthed expression, smiled briefly and carried on. "The reason I lost my temper was that the damned mannikin was so much like me, and I thought you had intended it as an insult."

"But I . . ."

"I know now, now I've thought it over. Do you think you could make as good a likeness of me again?"

"Er . . . I . . . well, I . . . er . . . I really don't know. That's the first thing like that I've ever done." Alonzo felt very flustered.

"Are you serious?" Silvander asked, frowning at him.

"Er, yes, well I've never made anything out of clay ever before. Well, I've never made anything out of

86

anything actually. I never had the chance."

Silvander stood, staring, turning the fingers of his right hand in and out of his beard and fingering his bottom lip. Alonzo thought that the look seemed to be going right through him to some scene somewhere off beyond his left shoulder. So strong was the feeling that he turned to see what it was that the big man was staring at.

Alonzo's move seemed to break the spell. "Come," said Silvander, taking him firmly by the elbow. "Let's see if you can do as well again."

They went back to the pottery and it was obvious that Turon had been listening and had almost been caught out by their sudden return. He was trying to start decorating a pot where he had left off halfway through and had made a very bad job of it.

Silvander ignored him, however, and said to the young King, "Use some of the lumps of clay you weighed up yesterday. Now, where do you want me to stand?"

"What?" said Alonzo.

"How do you want me to pose?" Silvander asked.

"I couldn't do it looking at you," Alonzo said. "I would hardly know where to start. Could I just do it as I did yesterday and see what happens?"

"Of course," Silvander said. "Do you mind if I watch?"

"Well, er, just this time, let me see if I can do it again on my own – if that's all right."

"Right. We'll get on with our own work. Just imagine it's yesterday and you're bored." Silvander laughed and moved over to his bench and wheel.

Turon was obviously pretending to be engrossed in decorating a new pot, so the young King picked up a chunk of clay, pinched some bits out to roll into sausage shapes, and started.

It was no problem at all. The figure seemed to make itself. Almost the only difference was that he knew he was going to be putting an apron on so this time he allowed for it, making the two little toes of the shoes first.

The caricature of Silvander's face was an even better likeness than the previous one, if that was possible. He had exaggerated everything. The nose was bigger, the eyebrows more woolly and the eyes even deeper set than they were in real life. The smile and the beard were amazingly life-like, especially in such a small figure. By the time it was all finished the potter was standing behind him, watching.

"I couldn't keep away," he chuckled, "and you were so intent on your work, you heard nothing." He laughed again. "That's me! Is that not me exactly?" He turned to Turon who was nodding his head.

"Now," Silvander was all businesslike again, "you get a small spoon and hollow out the inside of the body and the legs and up into the head, otherwise it will never fire."

"You want to fire this?" Alonzo was amazed.

"Of course. You have a great talent, young man. We'll fire it, and then I'll show you how to colour it and glaze it. Everyone knows me at the next Spring Fair and we could sell quite a few of these."

"Sell?" Alonzo stood open-mouthed. Here, at last, was something he could do that was *worth* something.

He could feel the heat in his cheeks, but this time he was blushing not with embarrassment, but with pleasure.

Alonzo found himself suddenly very popular. It became a mark of importance to have had your caricature done by this new "sensation". He found he couldn't do any sort of a portrait of anyone unless he had spent some time with them and got to know some of their characteristics, so he was suddenly everybody's friend.

Silvander's daughter, Lissia, who did all the colouring of the pots once they had been biscuit fired, was entrusted with teaching Alonzo all about how to achieve the various colours. But all the talk about glazes and colours, and how to create various effects like a "crackle" glaze, just seemed to wash over Alonzo. He had absolutely no interest in the next step. Once he had created the figure or figures all the life seemed to go out of him until he began the next project.

Lissia, or Lissi as she was called, was a bubbly, laughing girl of about fourteen or fifteen, and she seemed to know a great deal about everything to do with the glazes, the firing and the painting. In fact she was a very knowledgeable young girl indeed.

"She had to be," Turon explained one night as he strolled back with Alonzo from the pottery. "Her mother died when Lissi was nine. She was just a youngster but she hopped in and did all the cooking and washing and generally nursed old Silvander through his misery." There was a long friendly silence as they wandered along kicking the dead leaves from under their feet. Then Turon added, "I think he'd always wanted a boy to carry on the pottery, that's why he's taught her everything about everything. I should think you've put her nose right out of joint."

"*Me*?" Alonzo was amazed.

"Well, here you turn up, able to make all those things which she can't, and all she can do is colour somebody else's work. She's good, mind. Fine finicky detail . . . there's no one like her, and good ideas about colours, but it can't be much fun for her to hear her father praising you morning, noon and night. He thinks the sun shines out of your left nostril."

"Oh come on."

"He does, and the moon out of the other one. See if you can be a little more interested in Lissi's work and try and throw a hint of praise her way, you know? She's only human after all."

Alonzo walked along in silence. He was continually amazed at how much Turon knew and understood about the world and the people in it. Alonzo realised he had never had to consider anyone else but himself in his Palace upbringing. Maybe it was time he started to try.

As the days passed by, Alonzo tried to befriend Lissia, admiring her work and encouraging her. She flourished under his praise and as their friendship developed Alonzo was surprised by the lack of restraint shown in Lissia's dealings with him or any of the other men, and contrasted this starkly with the image he had of his own wife. He shook his head in amazement. That was another whole life away. It had been an arranged marriage and he had only met Alice a very short time before the wedding in a most formal and painful way. In time, they had become close, and Alonzo loved her dearly, and he was suddenly overcome by an enormous sense of loss and a longing to hold his wife to him in an intense embrace. He hunched his shoulders and tried to bury himself deeper into his jacket against the chill wind of the late Autumn evening as he returned to the camp. "I should move the bees," he thought to himself, "before the winter really sets in. They stand no chance unprotected when the snows come."

Alonzo had resigned himself to the fact that he would never see his wife again. What chance did he have of ever facing up to Count Tzlenko with all his power and saying, "Er, excuse me. You know me. I am the King. Could I start again where I left off, please?" It would be laughable if it wasn't so sad. The project of how he might shift the beehives kept his mind from dwelling on the despair in his heart.

Alonzo looked up to see a grave-faced Turon coming towards him.

"So you've heard," the lad said in some surprise.

"Heard what?" asked Alonzo.

"Oh, you haven't heard."

"Stop talking in riddles. Haven't heard what?"

"Well you looked so glum I thought you must have heard," Turon said. "Jentaro and his brother Jossuf have just returned from the capital, and the news is all over the place. There's been a proclamation, an announcement from the Palace . . ." He faltered to a stop. Alonzo was gripping him by the shirt front with both hands and his face looked dreadful. His nose was all sort of pinched-looking and very white, as was the rest of his face, the eyes, eyebrows and full beard and hair looking like dark patches splashed onto the pale background by some careless brush.

"What announcement?" the question from the King was so quiet that Turon nearly missed it.

"You're hurting me, Cockroach. Let go of my . . . thank you. Look, I can't help it. I'm just telling you what they were told."

"Which is?" the King's voice snapped out in a fierce whisper.

"Well," Turon took a huge breath and started again. "Well . . . Count Tzlenko has announced that he is going to be *King* Tzlenko in the absence of any offspring from the late King Alonzo and . . . I hate to tell you this . . ."

"Go on!" the voice from the very much alive King Alonzo sounded ghastly even to his own ears.

"He is leaving his coronation until the Spring Fair when the capital will be crowded and . . . I really hate to say this . . ." Turon's voice was getting quieter. He faltered, and eventually stopped.

"For God's sake tell me!" Alonzo's voice burst out, each word accentuated by a shaking grip of Turon's shoulders.

"I will, I will. He's going to marry her. It's going to be a huge celebration, a combined wedding and coronation and a special fair with competitions and prizes and he's cut most of the taxes by half and . . . well . . . he's going to marry the young widow of the late King Alonzo."

It was eerie. Turon's voice was joined by that of his friend so that those last four words were said in unison by the pair of them.

It had a very despairing sound to it . . . "The late

King Alonzo" . . . spoken by the King himself and by the only one in the whole Romany encampment who really believed that he was the King.

Alonzo let go of Turon's shoulders and slipped to the ground. His legs had just refused to support him.

When Turon knelt to comfort the King he could just make out the words "Alice, Alice," repeated over and over again.

Alonzo marvelled at how much he had learned from old Grigori the beekeeper in that one short day so long ago.

"If you're going to rob their house of honey, do it in the middle of a lovely sunny day, then all the workers will be away working," Grigori had said. "If it's thundery, don't go near them. Every bee left in the house will be upset and attack you. When it's fine, they almost help you steal the stuff." Grigori had laughed then. Alonzo could hear that thin, coughing sort of laugh in his head, as if it was happening right now.

"Don't use smoke unless you have to, and then, only a little. Too much smoke and every bee in the place starts eating up all the honey they can. They know that if it's inside them, no one, not even a fire, can steal it." Once again the cackling laugh from the old man.

Alonzo stood next to the caravan looking at the rope and sacking, the wedges made of wet clay and straw, and wondering whether it was too big a job for just himself and Turon. But everyone else was busy putting up the winter tent for the horses so they would just have to manage.

He had decided he must do something to take his mind off the misery of thinking over and over about the

Count and his own dear Alice. Why not move the bees?

He had gone over the old beekeeper's conversation in his mind, hoping he had missed nothing.

"If you're going to shift them," he had said, "they're funny little devils. You've got to take them at least four leagues away in one move . . . see . . . they can range easily two leagues from their house looking for blossom, and if they recognise the territory – and they're not stupid, you know – well, they'll fly right back to where their house used to be, and when it's not there, they just fly round and round in the same place looking for it until they die. So you've got to get them right away to somewhere where they have to learn the country all over again."

So now, here they were . . . just two of them, the daylight fast fading from the sky, and quite a task ahead of them.

Grigori's voice kept on plugging away in his mind. "Doesn't matter how you wedge 'em in, a few will get out and attack – you've got to ignore them stings, young fella. Do it early evening when all the workers are back and they're just bedding down for the night otherwise you leave half of them marooned."

Alonzo was aware of how morose he had been since hearing the news of the joint coronation and wedding. He couldn't seem to smile or think of a single thing to say to anyone. Turon had stuck to him, he couldn't think why. He had stayed away from the pottery, snapped some cruel statement or other at Lissia when she had tried to offer the hand of friendship. He would have to apologise to her and her father some time, he knew that, but at the moment a black cloud of gloom seemed to be draped over his shoulders. There was a slow, burning rage building inside him with no way of him releasing that tension. In his mind he kept seeing the face of Count Tzlenko and wanting to smash it to a pulp.

Go back and challenge him to a duel? That would be suicide, the Count being the fine swordsman that he was. Alonzo's stomach was churning away like a sick, sour machine.

He forced himself to forget the Count and everything to do with the Palace and concentrate on the bees.

It was a fairly cool evening, which was good. The bees would be sluggish and from what Grigori had told him, they would get all furious at not being able to get out and the hive would heat up considerably. If it was a hot night a lot of bees could die of the added heat they created with their angry fighting to escape. Both Turon and the young King were wearing hats with netting and gloves and Turon was quite terrified. It said a lot for his friendship or perhaps for Alonzo's mood that the younger man had not complained once when told what he would have to do.

They walked up on tiptoe to the clearing and carefully put their bundles down on the ground. No words were needed, as they had gone over the plan time and time again on the outward journey.

They took the wedges they'd made of clay and straw and quietly and efficiently they stopped up the entrances to all the hives.

It was important, Grigori had said, for air to be able to get in through the tiny straws but equally important that you filled up with clay any spaces a bee could crawl through.

Alonzo then brought up the six lengths of sacking and the rope. With all the planning they had done, it worked like a charm. Cover a hive with sacking, then Alonzo would lift the whole hive gently off the ground while Turon, shaking with nerves and dreading the first sting, quickly secured the whole package with rope. His knife was out of his boot top and the rope cut and on they went to repeat the process five more times. One thing made it more nerve-racking and that was the change of sound from inside the hives when they were first lifted up. One moment it was a low-pitched comforting hum and the next instant it was up to a clamouring, outraged buzzing. Each hive picked up the sound and joined in even before being lifted, so by the time the two friends were straining to carry two hives each back to the caravan they were sweating with fear just from the sound. Grigori had said that bees smelled the fear on you. It must be so because the sound became even higher-pitched and louder, if that was possible.

The horse was very jumpy and Turon had to talk to him all the time and try to calm him down. By the time they had returned with the two final hives, old Petro was jerking his head from side to side, the whites of his eyes showing up in the darkness and they were both very glad they had tied him so securely to the tree.

The journey back was very strange. They felt they should hurry so that the bees weren't sealed in for too long, but they also had to restrain the old horse for fear the hives were jolted too much. They had prepared a place for the hives to stand far enough away from the main camp so as not to be a nuisance, yet near enough that you could keep an eye on them. Grigori had said you must make sure the place you put the hive down was the place it was going to stay. Then stings or no stings, you had to undo them and unplug the entrances as soon as possible. The minute they were released they would attack of course, no doubt of that, but Grigori had said you must not kill bees needlessly. They were only defending their homes and you would be killing the very creatures that would be collecting honey for you again as soon as they calmed down.

Alonzo was amazed at how much he remembered, but then, thinking back, he realised it was the first time he had found himself really interested in anyone or anything. He was once again close to tears when he thought of the loss of the old beekeeper and then felt the bitterness welling up inside him when he thought of the man who was responsible for ending that friendship so soon after it had begun.

They arrived at their destination in the darkness just before dawn and the young King went about the task of unloading and positioning the hives, Count Tzlenko hammering away inside his head, firing his rage to even higher heights.

Turon was worried sick about unplugging the hives so Alonzo insisted that he should get away from them as soon as he had cut the ropes. The young Romany needed no second telling. Away he scurried to watch from the edge of the clearing as Alonzo grimly peeled away the clay and straw plugging each entrance. In an instant the bees were all over him, buzzing furiously, four or five deep over his clothes and the netting so that he was virtually blind. He brushed the net clear so that he could see to find the next hive, ignoring the odd bees that got inside his gloves and between his neck and his coat to sting him. In a way the pain just made him more angry with Count Tzlenko.

He found he was working automatically now, and when he became aware of the new smell, he honestly had no idea what it was. It wasn't until most of the bees had dropped from him in their smoke-induced stupor that he turned and saw Turon working away, squeezing the bellows on the smoke machine. The Romany lad had remembered their plan.

"Good!" Alonzo coughed his thanks to his friend, and making sure that the hives were all properly positioned and opened, he led the young Romany, still working away on the smoke machine, as he stumbled backwards towards the caravan.

Luckily the bees, concentrating on their tormentor, had ignored Petro, and Turon was able to then lead the old horse back to camp while Alonzo took over the smoke machine to work a rear-guard action. The stunned bees would recover soon enough and seek out the familiarity of their own hive, Alonzo was sure of that. He was also sure of one other thing.

"What's the name of that swordfighter who did such a good job on me?" he said.

Turon stopped and turned to look in amazement at the young King. At that moment the first light of dawn filtered through the mask of the beekeeper's veil, and Turon was stunned by the bitter, determined look on the haggard face of his friend.

7

Gascon stood looking at Alonzo trying to see how and where the change had taken place. The last time they had met he had felt he was facing an overgrown child intent on committing suicide. Now, there was an iron determination somewhere just below the surface.

"Well," he started, "if you're sure you want . . ."

"I'm sure," Alonzo cut right across his words, "just show me how."

"Huh," the word carried a million meanings, as did the slightly raised eyebrows and the pursed mouth. The very attitude of the swordsman seemed to say, "You're wasting my time – I've seen your sort before . . . blow hot . . . blow cold!"

Gascon made an effort to get hold of himself mentally and ignore the apparent rudeness of the man before him. He had been asked to teach the young man not only to defend himself but to perfect all aspects of attack as well. When he had been told the deadline for all this he had laughed out loud.

"The Spring Fair! Lord's legs . . . his feet'll never touch the ground. Does he know what he's asking?"

Now he repeated the question.

"Do you know what you're asking? You'll be tired like

you've never *been* tired. I seem to remember you're right-handed? Well, your right thigh muscles in particular are going to scream at you, in fact both legs will be murder all day and most of the night for at least a month. You'll be living and *dreaming* lunges, parries, ripostes . . . and how you'll hate me. You will *hate* me! Are you ready to take all that on?"

"I have a deeper hatred inside me that drives me to do this," Alonzo said. "Can we begin?"

"You will need to be a very determined man . . ." Gascon started, but Alonzo's curt nod seemed to say, "Enough of the advice, get on with it."

Gascon started again. "So, I'm assuming you know nothing, never had lessons . . ."

Alonzo cut in, "I *had* the basic lessons but I acted the idiot and learned nothing but a few Italian and French names, and I can't even remember what they're for. Start from the beginning," and then he added, "please."

The two men exchanged a half smile and suddenly the tension and the slight feeling of animosity had been blown away.

"Well, if you're to understand anything of what I'm about to teach you, we'll have to go right back and learn all those French names. Don't forget though, fancy names or not, whether you've learnt in a French '*Salle*' or picked up your brawling from street fights, it's the same basic aim. Kill that other man before he kills you, you understand?"

Alonzo nodded.

"Let us make a start. '*En garde*' means 'defend yourself', I'm going to get you if I can, all right? Let's start with your stance. Take the rapier, that's it, hold it gently with thumb and first two fingers, good. You can see that the cup-shaped guard protects your hand from the point of the blade . . . that's important . . . the *point* – that's the bit that's going to do the damage. Now, just watch this. All I have to do is lunge and I've skewered your elbow with the point of my blade."

The tip of Gascon's rapier had stopped just a fraction short, but Alonzo jumped as if he had been stung. There was a sudden burst of heat all over his skin, mainly from fright, but also from anticipating the awful pain of those two shoulder wounds all over again.

"You see, that's the first thing you learn – keep the target area as small as possible – you must *not* have your elbow showing. Keep your arm directly behind that guard. I'm sorry to have frightened you, but you should know how much work you have to do before a counter move becomes instinctive." Gascon paused. "Do you still want to learn?"

Alonzo nodded, his face white.

"Right, let's look at your stance. You position yourself almost edge on to your man so he sees as little of your body as possible. Do it – good – this right knee is bent slightly, see . . . if you stand flat-footed with legs straight it takes you much longer to leap into attack or to escape backwards from any attack. That's right. Point your right foot straight at him, good. Your left leg is also slightly bent but that foot should point straight out to the left side. Now . . . try this. From that position you can step forwards a bit at a time or backwards in the same way."

Alonzo tried the move and could see how the bent legs and the foot positions would keep you ready to go easily either forwards or backwards.

"Now, stand up, don't make any move, rest your weapon on the ground. I want you to see that bent position really working."

Suddenly Gascon gave a grunt and lunged forward. His back foot stayed where it was, but the front foot jumped a good yard forward and Alonzo gasped as he realised that from that standing position Gascon could have driven the rapier right through him. The swordsman looked up at him, smiling. His head was almost on a level with Alonzo's hip, his elbow was actually touching Alonzo's side and his hand and the whole of the rapier were well past Alonzo's body.

Gascon was not even breathing heavily. Maintaining his position with all his weight taken on the bent leg he chatted in a seemingly effortless way. "You've got to keep at it until you can do this seven hundred times in one practice session. I mean it, seven hundred times. Look at this back leg. You see the knee is almost touching the ground, but if I miss my man I can recover and even retreat," and he matched his action to his words, jumping his front foot back until he was upright again and then doing a further series of rapid jump steps backwards.

Alonzo stood staring at him, trying to take it all in.

"You still want to do it?" Gascon asked.

"I *have* to do it," Alonzo's voice had the pent up bitterness of all the past months.

"It will be hard then, make no mistake. Is that enough for a start, or can you take in more?"

"More!"

There was a look of grudging admiration from the

swordsman. He took a deep breath.

The next hour was spent going over and over the attack moves and when screaming point was reached, over and over yet again! Finally Gascon called a halt.

"That's enough for a start," he said. "Spend as much time as you can doing all those things. Don't forget, when you advance or retreat you must be instantly able to do either, that means you have to have your weight directly above the centre point between both your feet. Never get out of balance. Knees bent and you can jump either way instantly, instinctively! Right, I'll change that rapier for this wooden practice sword." The look on Alonzo's face stopped him mid-word. He took a deep breath. "You're right of course. Keep the rapier. Take care of it then. When do you want to see me again?"

Alonzo shrugged. "I don't know . . . would tomorrow be too soon?" Gascon started laughing and eventually the young King joined in. It was the first time he had relaxed since he had heard the news of the impending coronation and wedding.

The teacher clasped the pupil by both shoulders in a friendly gesture and realised too late that the old wounds still hurt a little. He pulled an apologetic face and stepped back.

"Practise all that and I'll see you tomorrow," he said and turning, he gathered up his bits and pieces and made his way back in the direction of his caravan. The casual observer would have noted that, as soon as he was out of sight of the young King, he cut sideways and made his way quickly and quietly round to a point of vantage to watch in grudging approval as his young protégé went endlessly over and over all the moves he had learned.

So began in earnest the training of King Alonzo IV. The days were to be the longest Alonzo could ever remember. Step forward, attack Gascon's *sixte*, watch the effortless parry executed in slow motion. Step back, try to anticipate the attack and try to parry, moving Gascon's rapier away past *quarte*. Start again. After that had been filed away in the King's mind and, in a way, in the muscle memory, they began on the next position, that is, turning the tables and parrying from *sixte* down and away through *septieme*, rather than sideways to *quarte*.

They had a brief respite and a drink of cold water. Alonzo noticed Lissia watching him from the trees. How long has she been there? he wondered. Gascon turned to see what Alonzo was looking at.

"Clear off, Lissi. He's enough to think about without you distracting him." Lissia turned and was gone. "Come on, let's continue," Gascon said, turning back to Alonzo.

This time Gascon showed him the attack to *quarte* and how it should be parried downwards past *octave*. This one Alonzo found devilishly hard to do.

When he had totally fumbled the parry for the tenth time Gascon stopped.

"I'm only pushing you because you've set me so little time. I think the first two are all your brain and muscles will take today. Let's run through them again until exhaustion stops you and we'll look at *quarte* to *octave*, and finally *octave* to *septieme* another time, suit you, Kosta?"

"Suits me fine, Gascon!"

Alonzo smiled at the grinning teacher. Being called Kosta made him feel very good inside. The children had found 'Konstantin' too much of a mouthful and shortened it, so now, whenever he was called Kosta, it reminded him of their acceptance of him.

Alonzo came over the rise and stopped in open-mouthed amazement. Every child in the place it seemed had a sword made of something: willow branches, bits of stick, anything that did the job and they were all lunging back and forth shouting *"En garde"*, *"sixte"*, *"quarte"*, *"sept"*, and a lot of other things, mostly unintelligible. On seeing their hero they all stopped and turned towards him. Every face was ready to burst into laughter, but there was an edge of uncertainty. The "King of the Kids" had been very moody of late.

Alonzo was exhausted and their eager faces gave him such a lift. He dropped the rapier, held out his hands towards them and laughed – he couldn't help himself. In the space of a heartbeat they were all over him, giggling and shouting and he was suddenly terrified that someone would break the weapon.

In the end, one of the twins grabbed it and held it up out of harm's way.

"Careful of the point," Alonzo shouted to make himself heard, "that can *kill* you!"

"It's safe with me, Kosta."

"Don't play with it. You can have someone's eye out." Alonzo was quite stern, "Face the point down. That's it . . ." Then he turned and smiled again. "Still friends, are we?" he asked and a couple of the youngsters made silly dogbarks and soon everyone was laughing as they jostled to get next to him and drag him back to the camp. His legs were aching and he was bone weary, but their enthusiasm carried him along.

Turon was the first one he saw when they got there.

"How fares the great swordfighter?" he asked.

"Dead tired," Alonzo replied.

"Not too tired to eat, I hope. Silvander's sent over to invite you. Lissi's cooked something special, I gather."

"I've upset her, I'm afraid," Alonzo pulled an embarrassed face. "I should apologise, I suppose, but I don't really know what it was all about."

"I think she thinks she's in love." Turon spoke so quietly Alonzo only just heard him over the chattering of his escort. He spun round to face his friend.

"But she . . . I . . . you don't seriously . . . she's only . . ." Alonzo's face burnt in those two telltale blotches.

"Surely you must have guessed?" Turon asked.

"No, I didn't. It's ridiculous. She's only a child."

Turon looked at him with all the wisdom of his fifteen years. "That's when it hurts the most, Cockroach."

It was an awkward meal. He had first apologised to Silvander for deserting the pottery. The old man had accepted the apology and said, "I understand. You've got other things on your mind, but you should make a little time each day to make some more figures. I'm going to do a gigantic firing soon and the more you have to sell at the Fair the better. You have great talent, my son, don't throw it away."

"It's just that I don't know if I can do it any more," Alonzo admitted something that had been in his mind for days now. "I have a bitterness in me, and . . . I don't know . . . I think you need friendship and happiness inside you to make the figures come alive."

"Maybe it's the other way, my boy. The joy of working in clay may be the thing that will chase the anger away. Try tomorrow."

"I have to practise with the sword," Alonzo said.

"But all day? No . . . surely. We have a saying . . . 'All work . . .' "

Alonzo finished it for him, " 'And no play makes Jack a dull boy.' I know the saying." Old Roger had used it when he was growing up but in a slightly different way. He had added, "But the reverse is even more important, all play and no work will make you a fool, my little prince." This was when he had refused to learn riding and acted the clown through his swordfighting lessons. If only he had listened. He jolted back into the present and became aware of Silvander waiting, expecting him to say something more.

"You're right," he said, "I'll try and fit in some time each day, yes . . . you're right."

Just then Lissia came through with the meal which was a mouth-watering stew, and Alonzo realised he was ravenous. The stew was very rich and there was fresh bread to mop up the golden fat which beaded the top of the bowl and afterwards a glass of homemade brandy to "cut the fat" as Silvander said. During the meal Lissia said never a word, kept her face looking at her food and just ate. The atmosphere sat very heavily on any conversation and the time passed slowly. Eventually it was over and Silvander said, "Well, you two will have a lot to talk about . . ." Alonzo looked at him open-mouthed. ". . . So why don't you go out for a walk and I'll clean up here."

107

"No, I'll do it – let me do it – it's the least I can do – lovely meal," Alonzo tried valiantly, but Silvander shooed the two out into the sharp coolness of the evening and shut the caravan door.

The awkwardness continued. Lissia walked slightly ahead, still looking down and Alonzo felt compelled to follow.

"Lissi . . ." Alonzo tried to start. Immediately the girl stopped walking and Alonzo stopped too. There was a terrible silence. Alonzo was aware of the coldness of the night. She started talking, her head still facing the ground and he had to move closer to try and hear what she was saying.

"What?" he said. " I didn't hear a word you said."

The Romany girl turned and Alonzo realised she was now too close, but before he could move back she dropped her forehead to touch his chest and murmured, "You think I'm too young."

"N-no . . . it's not that . . ." he stammered.

"Lots of girls get married at fourteen," she continued. "You like me, don't you?"

"I . . . er . . . well . . . yes, of course, I *like* you . . ." he tried to put a wealth of meaning into the word "like", but she seized on it.

"And I *love* you, and I'm sure you could grow to love me. If you like me, it's only a matter of time, and I know all about what people do and you could show me. My father likes you and he would be only –"

"Stop!" Alonzo was blushing furiously. He took hold of her shoulders to lend strength to what he was about to say, but she misunderstood the movement and flung her arms around him, still not looking up.

108

"Lissi . . . dear Lissi," he disentangled her arms, "it's not possible. I have a wife."

She shot back as if scalded, her shocked white face turning up to his. Her eyes were huge in the darkness and he watched them fill with tears.

"How could you?" she shuddered. "I hate you! I hate you!" and she beat briefly and furiously on his chest with her fists before dashing away, sobbing into the night.

He turned sadly and headed back to Silvander's caravan. When the potter opened the door Alonzo said, "I've upset your daughter – not knowingly – but I have upset her terribly. I feel I must tell you who I really am

109

and explain my situation." They stood and looked at each other.

Eventually Silvander said, "Where is she?"

"She went off crying up into the woods. I think it would be best if you went to her. She needs some comfort." The big man nodded. Alonzo continued quietly, "I'll wait here for you."

"You're a good lad," the old man said as he flung a mantle around his shoulders. "I'll be back presently."

Later that night, after he had told his story to Silvander, Alonzo lay, unable to sleep, his whole being full of a million thoughts, all tumbling over themselves and mixing with memories which replayed themselves in his head. Of course, they hadn't believed his King story, well, not at first, although Silvander had heard some rumour of it from the Council members. But it had been treated as a joke and laughed away at that time. Now, at last, they had believed him, and in a strange perverse way Lissia was somewhat relieved to find him so bitter towards his wife. She took solace in the fact that he couldn't bear the thought that she would agree to marry the Count. You could almost see her thinking that if she just bided her time, the young King would turn to her for comfort.

"Am I stupid?" Alonzo said out loud to himself in the darkness. Surely he would be sensible to do that, cut himself completely from his past life. Lissia would make a loving wife, and Silvander obviously eyed him favourably as a son-in-law. He would inherit the pottery . . . and then the image of the butchered Grigori came tumbling out of the darkness and stopped him. That gentle,

110

generous old man done to death by the ambitious murderer who was at this moment probably living as man and wife with *his* Alice and was planning to take over *his* throne at the earliest opportunity. He felt a hatred for them both, the Count and his own wife, and he could not rest until he had settled matters. It was no use – he must carry on with his sword practice and try to take back his Kingdom before the ceremonies at the Spring Fair. His decision made, he was able eventually to fall into a fairly troubled sleep in which he dreamt of a wife whose face was constantly changing to that of a heartbroken Romany girl.

"Six hundred and thirty one, six hundred and thirty two, six hundred and thirty three, six hundred and thirty four . . ." Alonzo's voice was a mere whisper as he counted off the lunges one after another. He was amazed at how good he felt. He was in terrific condition. Thinking back to the novice who was exhausted trying to get to *thirty* lunges on his first session he could not believe he was the same man. "Six hundred and forty nine, six hundred and fifty . . . Only fifty to go," he thought. "Six hundred and fifty one . . . six hundred and fifty two . . ."

Alonzo and Gascon had become very close over the month of daily gruelling swordfighting instruction. The older man had begun to open up about his past life and the young King was an avid listener, soaking up anything that might teach him more about the art of swordfighting.

Gascon had been a soldier in a crack French regiment and one of the best swordsmen in that regiment.

Duelling had been virtually banned by Louis XIV after one of his favourite courtiers had been called out and killed in a duel, but it still went on in clandestine bouts. From what Alonzo could gather, Gascon, or Gascon de Severigny, to give him his full name, the son of a Corsican nobleman, had been regarded as the best swordfighter with the rapier and a very close second in sabre fighting to one of the other officers of the regiment, and the trouble erupted when Gascon's promotion came through. The Comte de Bouveray, the officer in question, had always hated Gascon, referring to him as "that swarthy Corsican upstart", when Gascon was always just out of earshot. One day he had called him a "Corsican gypsy dog" to his face. Gascon had responded with a backhanded blow to the man's cheek and satisfaction was demanded. Of course it was unheard of for soldiers of different rank to fight one another, but now that Gascon was also a major, there was no barrier, and the duel took place in a remote farmyard one frosty morning.

Gascon had been toying with a new sort of defence which could have a sting in the tail. It involved appearing to give way when your opponent was binding your blade but in fact, not backing away with your body. Gascon had reasoned that he could allow his opponent's own strength to defeat him by backing away with his sword only, as it were, bending his elbow so that his arm moved left across his own body. As soon as his adversary's point had passed harmlessly to the left of Gascon's body, he had but to direct his own point correctly and, if his theory was right, his opponent should run himself right on to Gascon's blade. He would then only need to straighten his sword arm and the fight *should* be over.

The theory worked only too well. It was one of the shortest duels anyone could remember between evenly-matched opponents. Everything happened just as Gascon had imagined and the Comte was dead before he hit the ground, Gascon's rapier protruding a good two feet from the middle of his back. Gascon had let go of his sword as if it were suddenly molten metal and had stood there in white-faced disbelief. This was the first man he had ever killed and mixed feelings of horror and dread swept over him.

Retribution followed swiftly. Gascon was stripped of his rank and cashiered from the service. The outraged, powerful de Bouveray family then demanded the death penalty and Gascon fled just moments before the arresting officers arrived. From there he went into hiding, his life totally in ruins.

The law had lost him, but not so the de Bouverey faction. He was tracked down by a paid team of ruffians and beaten to within an inch of his life, only the arrival of a group of Romany caravans saving him as the would-be assassins fled.

It had been Orlando's father who had been in charge of those caravans at that time. This was some years before he had been elected Shero Rom but he was, even then, a figure of authority, and he had ordered his men to try to save the life of the battered and bleeding soldier.

Gascon's slow convalescence had lasted until well after the four caravans had travelled the breadth of Europe, and he was eventually adopted by the Romany band and had been with them here ever since.

"Six hundred and seventy two, six . . . seventy three
. . ." It was taking longer to recover now after each
lunge, his legs were almost beyond pain, they hurt so
much. He knew if he stopped working and straightened
up now his leg muscles would go into the most terrible
bout of shakes. He had had it happen before when he
stopped suddenly. The trick, he found, was to keep
moving, even if only gently, but at least keep the
muscles working and ease up gradually.

"Silvander's idea was a good one," Alonzo found his
mind wandering as the boredom of the repeated
exercise got to him. He had tried to go back into the
pottery as often as he could get time from the sword
training, but he found that his figures were all of doom
and gloom. The first thing he had made was old Grigori
as he remembered seeing him all hacked about and lying
sprawled and dead in the road in front of his hut. The
picture was so clear in his mind that the figure almost
seemed to make itself. He had such a black mood on him
that day in the pottery. He could remember how
shocked old Silvander had been by that figure and by the
group representation he had done of the horsemen in a
ring, swords raised, surrounding the helpless old man.

Somehow that had got a little of the bitterness out of
his system, and subsequently he had done a beautiful
portrait of old Grigori as he had first seen him and then
another one of him wearing the fateful wig and patched
jacket that had brought about his death.

Alonzo stopped dead in his tracks. The feeling of guilt
that overwhelmed him when he thought of the senseless
killing and the feeling of rage that wiped out all other

114

feelings left no room for counting lunges or practice of any sort. He stood stock still, staring into the distance, seeing the hated face of Count Tzlenko and striving not to couple it with the face of his young wife. But try as he might the images flashed back and forth of the Count fawning attendance and his dear sweet Alice looking up lovingly. The young King shook his head to try and banish the mind pictures and even scrubbed at his eyes with the knuckles of his left hand. His legs started to shake with the exhaustion of training and he sat down in an untidy heap on the ground.

Straightaway his left leg cramped and he had to thrust it out and pull back on his toes to straighten out the bunched up muscles. He then slowly lay down on his back and stared up at the top of the big winter horse tent.

A few horses ambled a bit nearer in their curiosity but most of them were used to this man's strange antics by now, and ignored him completely.

What was it he was thinking about before? Ah yes . . . Silvander's idea. It was a good one and if only Alonzo could make some sort of secret contact with old Roger, it might work. The vague plan was to have Roger leave various pottery figures in vantage points around the Palace so that they would be found, hopefully by the Count, or at least they would be brought to the Count's attention by whoever did find them. These figures would be of Grigori and his murderers, of the Captain of the bodyguard, of the murdered chef and his two dead assistants, and eventually of the young King himself. Alonzo had embarked on the making of all these figures with grim determination. In the same way he had produced Silvander's caricature, Alonzo let his visual memory take over. The final two were masterpieces, if he did say so himself.

One showed the young King, clean-shaven, sword in hand, striking the Count across the face with a glove, challenging him to a duel. The last one showed the horrified Count, eyes wide in disbelief as Alonzo's sword ran him through, while his own sword passed uselessly to the side of Alonzo's body.

Old Roger, if they could make contact, had but to hide these figures in the secret passageway under the Palace and bring them out, one at a time.

Silvander believed that this would play on the Count's superstitious fear, destroy his judgement and cause him to lose sleep and hopefully fill him with panic and terror.

The groups of figures had all been finished and they were about to be biscuit fired. Alonzo had to admit that if *he* were the guilty party they would certainly destroy *his* peace of mind.

As soon as the new figures were biscuit fired Lissia was going to colour them and put on the glaze and Silvander was planning a special small firing for them. The plan seemed to be marching forward inevitably. Even if he wanted to stop it now Alonzo doubted if he could.

As a result of Silvander's faith in him, everyone in the camp now believed him to be the wronged King, and Gascon, the Corsican, ex Parisian, ex-soldier, probably the most sophisticated and worldy-wise one in the whole encampment, had come up with an idea.

It was such a simple idea that it *had* to succeed.

116

8

The plan was that every Romany, whatever he or she was doing, would hint that a supernatural thing was going to happen. Romany women reading palms or tea leaves or telling fortunes would just happen to mention that it had been "seen in the stars" that the young King Alonzo would come back "from the dead" to claim his throne from the tyrant.

When pressed for further details everyone was to go tight-lipped and say they weren't supposed to have passed on this clairvoyant secret, only hinting darkly that the awful conflict would take place some time around the Spring Fair.

There is nothing ordinary people love more than passing on some illicit secret they aren't supposed to know about, and already the rumour was quite widespread. The Romany men were doing their part too, dropping hints that their womenfolk were seeing into the future, muttering things about the Phoenix arising anew from the ashes (an obscure reference to the supposed cremation of King Alonzo IV which every peasant would understand).

Alonzo lay on his back in a semi doze, smiling about Gascon and thinking what a clever man he was, and so was quite unprepared for Turon who was suddenly unlacing the tent flap in a frenzy, shouting, "Kosta, quick . . . Look out, Cockroach! . . . Where are you?" He burst in. "Malgordo's back . . . My God, Kosta, arm yourself, he's murderous!"

Alonzo couldn't seem to jolt himself out of this lethargy. The name Malgordo meant nothing to him. He dragged himself up onto one elbow looking in stunned amazement at his friend.

Suddenly it was too late. A flurry of running footsteps and a huge figure, muffled in cold weather clothing, appeared in the tent opening and Turon was knocked aside.

Alonzo couldn't ever remember seeing anyone look more menacing. The man was some years older than him. He guessed he'd be about twenty-seven or eight, swarthy-faced with a full black beard. His hair was covered with a sheepskin leather cap pulled right down against the cold and the heavy black eyebrows almost obliterated the glittering eyes beneath.

"The King, is it?" he spat out. "You might fool everyone else but not me, you miserable bed bug!" He laughed, a short, barking sound. "I'll teach you what it means to interfere in a Romany's betrothal promise!"

He covered the distance from the tent flap to Alonzo's feet in three huge strides and, too late, the King realised he carried a short stabbing knife in his right hand. That would have been the end of it but for the fact that Turon chose this moment to launch himself at the bigger man's back. There was a brief scuffle, long enough for Alonzo to galvanise himself into action, and suddenly the younger Romany was contemptuously

118

flung aside, a wicked gash below the thumb of his left hand, and Alonzo realised that Malgordo, if that was the name of this huge newcomer, was between him and his sword which he had casually laid on the ground some time ago.

Malgordo realised it at the same time, and a wicked smile spread across his face. "Steal my woman's affections, would you?"

He slashed at the King and it was pure luck that saved Alonzo. He kept jumping and circling, but the bigger man maintained his position between the King and his sword and had it not been for Turon, it would only have been a matter of time before one of the round-house sweeping dagger thrusts connected.

Suddenly there was a wild yell and about half a dozen horses came plunging in a startled group towards the two men. Turon was clinging onto the mane of one of the horses with his good hand and lashing out with both legs, kicking anything he could reach, yelling all the time. Malgordo had to give ground or be trampled and Alonzo was able to race round and snatch up his sword.

All of a sudden the scene had changed. Malgordo came charging back, jerking his own weapon from the scabbard at his waist and Alonzo realised with a cold shock in the pit of his stomach, that it was a sword, not a rapier. It would require all his wits to get him away from the slashing cutting edge of that heavy hunting sword, let alone the extra ever-present menace of the dagger which was now transferred to Malgordo's left hand.

Instantly he was under attack. The huge man raised his sword and cut down with it and Alonzo had only a split second to get his rapier up over his head in the

sabre parry Gascon had shown him. He caught the blade on the forte of his angled rapier but was totally unprepared for the ferocity of the blow. It would have split his head open had it struck home. As it was, his guard was bashed down and hit his forehead a stinging blow. For an instant he saw stars and to his shame he panicked and ran. All the bent knee positioning and lunging practice were gone. He fetched up in a cold sweat when the wall of the tent permitted no more escape.

Whirling about, he was just in time to make a clumsy parry which sidetracked the pointed end of Malgordo's sword. He was fast for such a big man and his forward motion carried his sword straight past Alonzo and through the hide of the tent wall.

Alonzo only just saw the flashing dagger blade and was able to duck and side step, unaware that he'd been cut. Once again he ran as fast as he could to an open space and turned. His heart was thundering in his chest and his breath was tearing great shuddering gasps from him. The huge Romany had dragged his sword back from the slit in the tent and was now swaggering slowly towards Alonzo with his teeth bared in a ghastly grin. It was his first mistake. It gave Alonzo a chance to get a grip on his fear and to plan something.

"Cold and calculating wins the day." He could hear Gascon's words. "Swift but not hasty" and again, "Think, Kosta, think!"

Suddenly he recalled the other overhead sabre parry Gascon had mentioned in passing. What had he said? "From this position you could easily decapitate your man."

Malgordo's sword came up for another murderous

121

attack and Alonzo was ready for him. The parry looked and felt awkward with his upper arm right across his body, shoulder under his chin, but he caught the sword exactly where his guard and the blade met, at the strongest point of his rapier. This time he was prepared for the strength of the blow and as the sword bounced off his angled rapier, he made a round house sideways swipe which would have taken off his opponent's head had he been using a sabre. As it was, the blade hit Malgordo right across the side of the neck with all the force Alonzo could muster.

Luckily for the big man the upturned leather collar took the brunt of it. Even so, it was an agonising blow. He gave an animal yelp of pain and clapped his sword hand up to his neck. He had momentarily forgotten his opponent which was a foolish thing to do, and his second mistake.

Everything seemed to slow down for Alonzo. He had all the time in the world to recover and he seemed to be standing outside himself watching as he went into the well-practised manoeuvre for the lunge.

The arm began to straighten, the foot kicked up into the forward step and he watched the point of his sword move slowly into the material of the Romany's jacket where it covered the pectoral muscle. At the end of the huge step he straightened his arm and felt the point of the blade grate against the bone of the shoulder blade and turn aside slightly to burst out through the material at the back of the jacket.

Suddenly everything jolted back into normal speed. He recovered, dragging his rapier back out of his assailant, watching the bloodstain spreading and flinching at the sound of the high-pitched scream.

He realised in shock that the noise was coming from Malgordo. The big man was as white as a sheet. His cap had fallen off as he sank to his knees and the black hair gave a shocking contrast to the colour of his face.

Alonzo turned in a daze to see all the camp, it seemed, crowding in through the tent flap.

Turon, holding his cut thumb in his mouth to stop the bleeding, was looking up at him with hero-worshipping eyes. They exchanged smiles and the King just had time to whisper, "Thanks, my friend, you saved my life," before everyone else was around him.

Gascon was there, sword in hand and he took the King by the back of the neck and dragged him into a rough embrace.

"I came expecting the worst but you didn't need me. First blood, my young fighting rooster. How do you feel?"

Alonzo looked at him, unable to say anything as his legs started to shudder under him and finally gave way altogether.

"My parents and his parents were really good friends and when I was born on Gordo's thirteenth birthday they took it as a good sign, an omen . . . so we were betrothed." Lissia paused and turned to Alonzo. "They did that sort of thing a lot. In a small community like this there are strict rules as to who you can and can't marry. The girl has no say of course, she has to do as she's told."

"So what changed it all?" Alonzo asked.

"It was Gordo himself. When he was . . . what? . . . I

would have been nearly two years old, so that would make him close to fifteen, their horse and caravan were swept away trying to cross a flooded river. Gordo was left on the bank looking after half their belongings that they'd off-loaded, to make the caravan lighter I suppose, and he had to watch them drown. It must have been awful for him. He was such a strong boy and to be standing there helpless . . . awful." She turned from packing in the last of the sawdust around the figures.

"He hardly spoke for about a month and then he went very strange. He felt everyone was looking at him and he started fighting. He was such a big man as you must know, and everyone began to avoid him. If he caught anyone looking at him, he would just go crazy and pick a fight, and he always won. That's when everyone began calling him *Mal*gordo. Of course the more people avoided him, the more perverse he became. Eventually he teamed up with a gang of horse-breakers at one of the Spring Fairs and that was when I was about five, so I don't remember much about it. But he was exactly right for them, very strong, kept to himself, did his work, always ready for a fight, or so I'm told, and he took off, following the fairs and the carnivals and we didn't see him again until I was about eleven, I suppose. He came back expecting to marry me. But of course we'd lost my mother by then and my father wouldn't hear of me heading off with him as his camp cook and maid of all work, and they had a most fearful row. I can remember it as clear as day. I was hiding in the sleeping berth and they were shouting and he drew a knife on Daddy."

"A nice way to impress your future father-in-law," Alonzo laughed.

"It wasn't funny, Kosta, he was beyond all reasoning. They were outside circling each other, knives drawn when the Shero Rom arrived and ordered them separated. Malgordo was manhandled by half of the men in the place. It was a dreadful scene. He swore he would be back for me and Daddy told him never to even come near me or he'd kill him. I was terrified, as you can imagine."

"And that was the last you saw of him?"

"Until yesterday." Lissia looked up at him shyly from under lowered brows and Alonzo felt his heart lurch.

"And you sent him after me?"

"No! I told him I was in love with someone else." Lissia looked at Alonzo and the illtreated-puppy-dog-look infuriated him in one way, but at the same time filled him with an urge to protect her against the world, a funny, mixed-up loving, annoyed feeling. "I had to tell him the truth, Kosta. I was terrified of him, but I didn't know he would find out that it was you. Honestly!"

That was yesterday. Here he was now, his shoulder all bandaged, sitting in the pottery watching Lissia as she set about firing his figures – the ones he planned to place in the Palace to unsettle the Count.

After the fight Silvander had forbidden him to do any work for a couple of days in order for his stab wound to heal, so there was nothing he could do to help. He now found the firing process fascinating though, wondering how sawdust packed in and around all his pottery could ever burn to the temperature needed to biscuit fire everything. It was a mystery. There were two holes left at the bottom for air to get in and out and then the fire bricks were built up into a sort of small dome shape,

125

standing the figures up in the central space and filling with sawdust as they went.

When she had packed the last of the sawdust into the top of the dome she poured a little bit of oil on the top, just enough to get the sawdust burning and then started a fire with the tinder box.

The last few bricks were all wedge-shaped to make the top of the dome. She fitted them in and then systematically went over all the bricks with a fairly sloppy buttery mix of clay so that the whole thing was airtight except for the two holes at the base.

Lissia checked and the top bricks were warm so that meant the sawdust was still burning. Soon the temperature would build up as the sawdust smouldered, fed by air sucked up from below.

"Why don't you light it at the bottom?" Alonzo asked.

"Burns too fast then – and don't ask me why, but that just doesn't do the job." Lissia gathered up all her things. "We should be able to crack the clay and open it up tomorrow night if it's cooled down enough. Then I can get on and colour them."

"I think the plain figures would do the job better, Lissi," Alonzo said, "and we really need them to start appearing in the Palace now and over the next month or so, to build up the fear in Count Tzlenko's mind. Anyway, it would take too long for you to colour them all."

Lissia was all indignant. "I colour them as fast as I can – you don't want rubbishy mass-produced things otherwise any of the *children* could do pink dots on cheeks and brilliant white teeth and . . ."

"I know, I know, Lissi. Don't get upset. I'm not

criticising *you*. I've just decided that plain terracotta-coloured will do the job and time is the important thing." Lissia started to put another point of view, but the King cut her off mid-word. "Look, don't argue. It's my Kingdom I'm trying to regain and that's the way I'm going to do it!"

Lissia gave a snort of disgust through her nose, turned and flounced out of the pottery.

Alonzo looked up to the heavens as if to say, "Save me from temperamental women!" and then kicked the wall in frustration at having upset the girl. The kick jarred his wound and he grimaced in pain.

He didn't want to follow after her and make the peace. It would mean backing down and changing the timetable he had planned in his mind.

"Huh! . . . Women!"

He wandered aimlessly about the camp. Everyone was busy making things for sale at the Spring Fair. Dorkus, the blacksmith, was fashioning wrought iron scrolls and elaborate door numbers and a few sample words spelled out in iron. He had made "Restaurant" and "Doctor" in the hope that he would get orders to make work over the *four* days the Fair would now run.

Alonzo felt he should go and see Malgordo, who was feverish by all accounts, but he didn't know what sort of reception he would get. Alonzo had become somewhat of a hero for subduing the big man. Malgordo had been a disruptive element every time he appeared at the camp. People were quite pleased to see him cooled down a bit. Alonzo thought he might go and see him when he got over his fever. "If he gets over his fever," he added as an afterthought.

Alonzo found himself down by the beehives and he sat down on the old tree stump. He had taken to going there quite often. There was a solitude there and also a companionship from the background murmur of the bees. Here, completely on his own, he felt he could easily commune with his beloved Alice. As long as no one was watching he could pour out his hopes, his fears and his plans as if she were sitting right there beside him.

"How could you even *think* of marrying that ghastly man? Alice, how could you?" He dropped his face into his hands and ignoring the pain from his shoulder he gave way to his emotions.

*   *   *

It was literally child's play for Alonzo to find the passageway.

Since he was first able to run around, old Roger had shown him this tunnel and it was their secret.

From what he could remember, it had been constructed by his ancestor King Alonzo II for some illicit purpose or other, and it ran from a hidden chamber near the wall of the Palace out to what had been the old woodcutter's hut on the edge of the forest. This place was now derelict, long since vandalised and burnt.

Alonzo had picked his way through the trees and creepers which now grew up through the blackened old flagstones of the floor, and Turon followed, hardly able to see a thing in the darkness of the night. They went down the disused steps into a foul-smelling cellar and Turon was guided into the entrance of the secret tunnel by Alonzo's hand. He never saw what the young King did to open the door, but the next thing he knew, his friend was striking a light from the tinder box and the beautifully constructed tunnel walls were revealed, stretching off into the gloom.

They moved off in the direction of the Palace, Turon still carrying the sack of pottery figurines, Alonzo leading with the flickering light.

"Steps down," the King's voice hissed. "Mind . . . it's wet underfoot here."

"Someone coming!" Turon blurted out. They stopped dead as Turon's voice echoed back, "Someone's coming!"

The King tried to suppress his laughter to no avail. "Sorry, Turon," he chuckled, "I should have warned you. I used to love to play pretend games up and down here with the echo of my footsteps."

Turon was a bit put out. He was nervous enough anyway with the whole undertaking and now his heart was thumping away behind his ribs and threatening to leap out of his chest altogether.

"It's not funny, Kosta. It scared the wits out of me!"

"I'm sorry, my friend," the King patted the young Romany on the shoulder. "I forget. I've known this place all my life, I forget it's all new to you. Come on. We're just going under the Palace wall now. From here on this was all cut through living rock. Must have taken them forever."

The situation between the King and the Romany had changed since the fight with Malgordo, and now it was even more evident that the King had become the leader, the decision maker, and the Romany the novice, the follower.

They were soon going up a circular staircase, also cut

out of the rock, and if Turon hadn't been so tense and nervous he might have marvelled at the craftsmanship of those Italian stonemasons of so long ago.

"This will be the tricky bit. Are you happy to wait here?" Alonzo's whisper was just audible.

"Not really, but I suppose I don't have any other choice. Are you going to be long?" Turon's whisper, try as he might to disguise it, had a shaky panic edge to it.

"I don't know. Everything depends on everything else. There shouldn't be any guards, there never used to be, but who knows? If old Roger's locked his door that'll be awkward."

There was a long pause, and Turon looked up to see what was troubling his King.

"What is it?" he asked.

"I just had a horrible thought. I don't know if the old man's still around. He could have died in the meantime. He's very old . . . oh my God, Turon, what if he's dead?"

"Come on, Kosta," Turon laid his arm across Alonzo's back and gave him a reassuring squeeze, "only one way to find out."

The King looked at his friend. How natural these Romanies were in their actions, their showing of affection. To a boy like himself, brought up never to touch or to be touched by anyone except old Roger, it was a constant surprise, and a very warming thing to feel a part of. "I'll wait," Turon continued, "I won't be happy till we're out of here and back in the caravan, but don't worry, I'll wait here for you."

Alonzo gave a nod, took a long look round the cramped chamber and then turned to the door-opening

131

mechanism. Inside here it was a simple matter of pushing a stone slab down with your foot and holding it down while you pulled the big pivoted wall slab towards you.

Alonzo had another sudden thought. "Could you bear to put the light out?" he asked.

"Oh no, Kosta . . . how long for?"

"Only until I'm out. See . . . if there *is* a guard, a light showing when the door opens will be the end of us. Soon as it's closed again you can light up, but watch this slab, and when it goes down to floor level that means I've pushed up the locking stone the other side and I'm coming back in, so you'll have to be ready and douse the light quickly again."

"What if it's not you that comes in?"

"Nobody else but Roger and I know about this tunnel. You're safe, no more talk. Light out. See you soon." These last words were just a whisper in the darkness. Turon strained to hear the opening and closing of the stone slab. His heart was once again thumping in his chest as he grabbed the tinder box and fumbled to get a light started. He was almost crying in panic and the feeling that he was entombed for ever in this Stygian darkness rushed in on him from all sides.

"Rodda . . . Rodda!" Alonzo was kneeling beside the old man's bed. He was using the old trick Roger had shown him for waking someone from a deep sleep without frightening them. Holding the old man's wrist between finger and thumb he squeezed gently.

"Rodda!" Once again he used a "put on" baby voice and whispered the name he had used as a little child

132

when he couldn't pronounce "Roger" correctly.

The old man stirred and sat up. "Come now, your Highness, it's much too late for you to be wandering around the castle. You should be . . ." He stopped mid-word. There was a moment of absolute silence and then the wrist was jerked out of Alonzo's grasp. "Who are you? What do you want of me?" There was a frightened quaver in the old man's voice.

"It's me, Rodda. You must have known I didn't die of food poisoning. I'm very much alive. It's *me!* Ask me anything. Things only I would know. Ask me!"

"My mother's name?"

"Gretchen." Alonzo fired the name back at him almost before the question had finished.

"Where was I born?"

"Rothenburg op der Tauber." Once again the answer cracked back.

"When did my family leave Germany?"

"The day after your fifth birthday . . . that would be the ninth of Oct . . ."

"It *is* you . . . it must be, my Lord. Saints be praised!" The old man started to weep and Alonzo grasped the frail shoulders to his chest.

"Come now . . ." His own eyes filled with tears and a huge lump seemed to well up in his throat. He could hardly talk. "You should be happy, not crying. There now. Get a cloak around your shoulders. I need you in the secret tunnel." He patted the old man on the back and helped him up. In the darkness they picked their way down the familiar corridors and passages and eventually lifted the bossed stone that released the slab from the outside. Alonzo waited for an instant to allow

133

Turon to extinguish the light inside and then pushed his way in.

"You all right, Turon? I wasn't too long was I?" he asked.

"Only about three lifetimes, Cockroach. Can I strike a light now?"

"Please."

A spark leapt in the darkness, then another and as soon as Turon had the geography of where everything was he got the tinder smouldering and in no time there was a little flickering flame.

"Turon . . . meet my dearest friend, Roger . . . Roger . . . Turon . . . he's my second best friend." This was addressed to the old man who stood shivering between them.

"You're cold, Roger."

"No, it's just been a bit of a shock. I must sit down." Roger subsided onto the floor. "Let me look at you, 'Lonzo. You've changed. It's not just that you're thinner and you've grown a beard . . . it's you. You're a man, my son. I'm proud of you."

They maintained silence for a few moments, the young man crouching, the old man sitting, arms extended and hands gripping hands.

"I love you, Roger. I've never told you." And suddenly the King was sobbing like a child and it was the old man's turn to do the comforting.

"Er . . . hm, hm." Turon cleared his throat noisily and then said, "Kosta, we should make a move. We must be well away from here by dawn."

"Yes, yes." Alonzo stood up, wiped his eyes, sniffed noisily, swallowed and said to his friend, "I'm sorry to break down. I never thought I'd see this dear old man again."

"You don't have to explain to me, Kosta. I'm a Romany. We know feelings. You do have to explain the plan, though."

"Yes." Alonzo turned to the old man and kneeling down, he outlined as quickly as possible what was required.

Roger nodded as he understood each new element of the plan and somehow refrained from asking all the questions he was burning to ask.

"I'll tell you the whole story later when there's time. The last thing is, you must, at the earliest possible chance, get a copy key made to the Count's bedchamber. Can you do it without getting caught?"

"I can but try. I should do it before I start leaving the figures."

Alonzo nodded. "Hide it in here, over in that old box under something, so that if suspicion does fall on you, I can still go ahead with the plan."

"Which is?" The old man's question hung in the air.

"Which is to challenge him to a duel to the death inside his own bedchamber."

"You'll be slaughtered, 'Lonzo."

"As you said earlier, Roger, I've changed. I'm a man now and I'm going to win my inheritance back by combat. I'm going to . . ."

"Kosta. I'm getting very afraid, we must make a move."

"Of course . . . just the blink of an eye and I'm with you," and Alonzo quickly unpacked the pottery figures from the sack Turon had carried, arranged them in the

135

right sequence, kissed the old man on both cheeks, embraced him and they were away down the spiral staircase in the middle of the stone floor. The old man slowly merged with the darkness as the source of light moved further and further away.

Finally there was a deep sigh, the sound of material

sliding over old parchment-like skin, a barely audible thud as the old man trod down the door-opening mechanism and an even darker oblong shape opened in the choking blackness.

The dogs started barking when they were still well away from the camp, but the jingling of the harness and the sound of Turon's special whistle turned it quickly into a "welcome home", rather than a "keep your distance" sound. The caravan was soon surrounded by a wagging tail brigade and the dogs accompanied them right back into camp. It was very late, maybe an hour or two hours at the most before dawn and both young men were exhausted and very cold.

Alonzo was shivering under his double layer of blankets and when Turon jumped down to lead the old horse the last part of the way Alonzo was so stiff with cold that his jump pitched him full length onto the frosty ground.

Turon turned and helped him up and the companionable laughter from the two just seemed to reinforce the bonds of friendship that had linked them almost from their first meeting.

Every breath sent up plumes of condensation in the cold pre-dawn darkness as the two set about unharnessing old Petro. The odd camp dog would come and nuzzle up to Turon's legs, get a pat on the head or have his ears tousled before wandering away as the friends tried to get their frozen limbs working again.

Petro needed no urging as he headed for the big tent. Once inside, the old horse went straight to the hay pile amidst welcome "nickering" from the other animals standing in the close warmth of the group. Turon and Alonzo took turns rubbing him down with handfuls of straw, drying off any sweat that might chill him later, and when that was done Turon threw his arms over the old horse's head and embraced him as they stood forehead to forehead.

Turon finally gave the trusty old horse a big kiss on the nose and a final pat on the forehead and then they were once again out into the bitter cold.

It had been a long and exhausting trip both physically and emotionally, the best part of two days used up in travelling in each direction, never knowing if the plot might be uncovered and foiled at any time, tension a constant companion throughout.

"Turon," the King turned his friend by the shoulder so they were face to face, "thank you for these last days, I could never have done it without you. If this works and I get back you'll be well rewarded."

"Hah," Turon was slightly embarrassed, and punched his friend playfully on the arm to cover it. "I don't need any reward . . . don't want any. Just keep up the sword work so that when we get you back in there, you win."

"Yes." Alonzo felt a fluttering of nerves at the thought of Count Tzlenko as he had seen him many times, sword in hand, reviewing troops, an awe-inspiring figure. Could he beat the man? He shook himself free of the doubts. He could only do his best and if he had anything to do with it, that "best" was going to be something to contend with, Count or no Count. The two friends embraced in the shoulder hug that Alonzo was slowly getting used to, and went their separate ways, Turon to his own family caravan for a well-earned rest, Alonzo to the sleeping berth he now used in the front of Silvander's caravan.

Silvander's was easy to pick out in the darkness because it stood slightly higher off the ground than the others around it. When the first snows fell the Romanies would shovel that snow under their caravans and tightly pack it into the space between the floor of the caravan and the ground. It sounded like a contradiction but this solid chunk of hard-packed snow provided a great insulation against the cold, mainly by stopping the winds from whistling past underneath. Alonzo looked for the highest patch of white and headed for it. That would be the snow under Silvander's caravan. He was dog-tired and still a bit shivery as he climbed the steps and tried to open the door quietly so as not to disturb Silvander and Lissia in their sleeping berths at the far end of the caravan.

Alonzo was too tired to undress. He planned to just collapse and pull the other blankets from the bed over him. He bent down to reach into his bed and his heart almost stopped with fright as his hand touched another cold hand in the darkness.

"God, Lissi, you frightened me!" His voice exploded in a hoarse whisper, "What are you doing, girl?"

"I couldn't sleep waiting to see if you'd get back safely and when I heard the dogs barking I knew it was you . . . I just knew. Are you all right?"

"Does your father know you're here?" Alonzo was beset with guilty feelings.

"No . . . he's still asleep."

"Lissi, you shouldn't be here."

"Don't send me away." Alonzo could just make out

the paleness of her face in the surrounding dark of the blankets.

"Lissi . . ."

"Did you see your wife? What did she have to say?"

Alonzo's mouth dropped open and his eyes opened wide in the darkness. In the tension of the four days since he had left the camp no single thought of his beloved Alice had crossed his mind. He could not *believe* it. He had not even enquired as to her welfare or her health when he saw old Roger. Perhaps subconsciously he had not wanted to know if his wife had in fact betrayed his memory and was actively and enthusiastically looking forward to the wedding. He knew he had dreaded finding out that they might already be living secretly in the Palace as man and wife, but that didn't excuse the fact that he had honestly not thought of her at all in the tension of that night in the castle.

"You never saw her?" Lissia asked, and when the young King could only manage a mumbled reply, she continued, "You've forgotten her!"

What instinct told her that? Alonzo thought, and he said, "Er . . . we were so busy, Turon and I, er, we never had a chance to . . ."

"Alonzo, it's me you want, you know it is. Alonzo!" And she threw her arms around his neck. Alonzo was staggered by the strength of the girl. It seemed as if his neck was breaking and he felt as though he was drowning in her hair, unable to snatch a decent breath.

"My god, Lissi, you're hurting me," he managed to force the words out against her shoulder. Lissia let go of him as if she'd been stung. "Lissi, put something on. You'll catch your death. We shouldn't be here like this."

His heart was thudding away like a crazy thing and the adrenalin was flooding through his system.

Lissia was clutching him to her again in a sort of wild desperation and kept muttering, "Don't send me away, 'Lonzo, don't send me away."

"Lissi, you must go back to your own bed. Please go . . . my dear sweet girl, please go, please." Alonzo's voice was a whisper.

"I won't go – don't make me." Lissia's face was wet with tears. Alonzo was backing away almost before he realised it. The door was just a step away. "Don't leave me like this. Where will you sleep?" Her voice followed him out into the night.

In the back sleeping berth, old Silvander lay wide awake, listening to his beloved daughter sobbing. How like her mother she was. He ached to go and comfort her, but in his wisdom he felt he should let her cry herself out.

Alonzo shuddered in the dark. He had never felt so cold in his life. Where could he go to get warm? He turned shakily towards the horse tent.

9

In the final month before the Spring Fair, Alonzo's sword practice moved up to a new tempo. Every day, for most of the day he worked with Gascon and now they were fighting in earnest. Some of the lunges and attacking moves on both sides had become really dangerous, so Gascon insisted they make foils to cover the point of each blade. It was a simple matter of getting some beeswax, warming it up a bit and rolling it, together with a lot of flaxen twine, into a ball. This was stuck right on the tip, and effectively "foiled" the blade, so that any "hits" from either man were not killing or wounding blows.

And so the pace hotted up. Gascon was concentrating on teaching Alonzo his "secret" move, his parry in which you appeared to give way when your opponent was binding your blade, but then redirected your point after sidetracking his. The first time Alonzo got it to work it felt miraculous. It was so easy that Gascon walked himself right onto Alonzo's point. The Corsican's eyes shot open in amazement. He hadn't realised how terrifying it would be to be on the receiving end. Had the beeswax foil not been there he would have been a dead man.

The two men stopped, and stood in open-mouthed amazement and suddenly the young King was laughing and clapping Gascon on the back. He couldn't believe he would ever get to a standard of swordsmanship where he would be tricking the master with such apparent ease.

"It worked!" he chortled. "Gascon, it worked!"

"It most certainly did, my young friend. Would you mind not battering my back like that. You're stronger than you think."

"I'm sorry," the King stepped back, slightly chastened, but still grinning all over his face and Gascon moved forward and hugged the man. He had grown to love Alonzo, and regarded him almost as the younger brother he never had.

"We'll get that well and truly into your subconscious so that it's an instinctive thing whenever a 'bind' is being put on your blade. That was good . . . that was *so* good, I couldn't *believe* it! We'll do it again and again, and then yet again! Come on, my young friend, one lucky hit doesn't make you the conquering hero." He chuckled, took up his stance and smilingly growled, "*En garde!*"

After the practice, Alonzo trudged over to the blacksmith's caravan to see Gordo. He was tired but had an inner glow that kept saying "Well done . . . you are good at something at last." He felt marvellous.

Dorkus was working at the anvil with the usual complement of youngsters watching the sparks fly, hoping to get one to land on their skin and give them that "fright". He nodded a welcome to Alonzo out of the corner of his eye as the young King opened the door of the caravan and went inside.

143

He wasn't really surprised to see Lissia there talking to Gordo, but there was still a twinge of jealousy in him. It was a strange feeling. He knew he had forfeited any claim on her feelings that night of the return from the Palace, but he realised he had liked the role of being her hero.

Big Gordo was recovering well. The depth of the wound meant that his right arm would always move slightly awkwardly, but since Lissia had been changing the dressings every day and keeping him company, the change in him was quite remarkable.

Alonzo knew that Lissia's first visits were engineered to coincide with his own, and he was aware that the outrageous flirting with the sick man was only done to make Alonzo jealous and possibly force him back into her arms in a more enthusiastic role.

What neither of them had realised was the effect all this would have on the big man and eventually on Lissia herself. In one of those about faces that so often happen in human relationships, she realised she quite liked Gordo and that the flirting was no hardship at all. Gordo of course revelled in it. He had always considered her to be his wife and was just biding his time until she was of marriageable age, and now she blossomed under all this attention.

This day when Alonzo turned up to see him, Lissia was already there. Gordo had had his hair and beard trimmed and washed and he really looked very presentable – nothing like the ogre he had first appeared to be. He appreciated Alonzo going to see him, but it was Lissia he really waited for each day. Now, as the King entered, they turned and smiled at him and he had to concede that they looked a handsome pair.

"Well, what did he say?" Gordo stood up.

"He says any time you think you're fit he'll go through some exercises with you. He doesn't know how much you'll be able to do with that arm, but he said you can but try, and he'll help where he can."

Actually Gascon had not said anything of the sort. He had not held out any hope for Malgordo ever being able to hold a sword properly again, and actually was not disposed to help at all. "The man's a bully and a thoroughly dislikeable, overbearing, nasty piece of work," he had said, "and I don't want anything to do with him."

"He's changed," Alonzo had said. "You'll see. For my sake, just put him through his paces once and see what you think."

Gascon had heaved a big sigh. "You strain the friendship, Kosta . . . all right . . . just one session."

"I'm sure you'll find . . ."

"Yes, *yes*. You drive me crazy sometimes. You get an idea and you won't let it go. You're like a dog with a bone. If persistence has anything to do with it you'll sweep that man out of the Palace like that!" And Gascon had snapped his fingers to end the conversation.

Now, as Alonzo looked at the awkward stance and the bandaged arm he felt that sweep of guilt he had so often felt during his visits.

"I'm so sorry, Gordo. I didn't . . ."

"I've told you not to mention it again. I got what I deserved. I just went mad that day and I'd have killed you if I could. You had to stop me and you certainly did that." He laughed. "Besides," Gordo continued, "if you hadn't spiked me, this girl of mine and I would probably never have got back together, so I already owe you more than I can say. Any time you need me – in a fight, anything, just say the word, big Gordo will be with you."

"Thank you," Alonzo said.

Gordo nodded his head. "I'm yours to the death," and he reached out his right hand, gave a quick wince of pain, and then laughed. "Maybe it's too early for sword lessons," he said, "but I've got to try."

"Gascon says whenever you think you're ready. I know *I'm* ready for a sleep! I'll see you two later." Alonzo made his farewells, exchanged a few pleasantries with Dorkus and the children on his way out and headed for bed.

He was exhausted.

The whole camp was on the move. Everywhere you looked there was a turmoil of packing. The big tent had long been folded away with the melting of the snows and the children delighted in running here, there and everywhere.

Alonzo loved the way the older Romanies involved their children in the day-to-day running of their lives. They never seemed to fob them off with childish things to occupy their time. It was as if each child was an adult, but a little smaller than the full-grown adults, and each child was given adult-type tasks suited to their strength and capabilities. They were learning about life all the time. The young King compared this approach to the wasted years of his own childhood where he had learnt nothing, except how to be a thoroughly unlovable, obnoxious little prig.

146

Alonzo laughed to himself. He had been down to the hives that morning and all seemed well there. The twins had taken down the snow roofs that had been built and had removed all the insulation straw from the hives. The bees were flying in and out quite happily. Alonzo guessed they had managed to find some blossom somewhere and were busy stocking up on honey again.

On the way down to the hives he had passed his old sleeping quarters – the rough windbreak he had first constructed when he was a virtual outcast with only the children, and Turon of course, as his friends. How he had changed since then. How *everything* had changed!

Yesterday he had gone through his final work out and as an added "spice", Gascon had arranged for big Gordo to enter the fight as a third party. This was really to see if Alonzo could instinctively parry and react with attacks coming from two different directions. Of course all the points were foiled and Gordo was still very awkward with his right hand, but he had taken to changing his blade to his left hand at critical moments and this was very confusing for an opponent. Gascon had finally called a halt.

"Well," he had said, "I can't do any more for you. I'll expect some sort of order when you're back on the throne . . . what do you think, your Majesty? . . . Protector of the Royal Personnage?" and they had all three of them burst out laughing.

"Seriously, Gascon," Alonzo had said, when the laughter had died away, "do you think I can do it?"

The Corsican looked at the young man standing so seriously before him.

"I would have liked you to have more experience with *real* fighting," he said. "From what you tell me, the Count is no novice where weapons are concerned, and he'll be wanting to put you away as fast as he can. His life and his future depend on it. I've tried to prepare you, but no amount of preparation will help you deal with his experience. A man like him, he'll have all sorts of dirty tricks up his sleeve. Beware of being manoeuvred back into chairs or tables or being trapped against a wall. Well . . . listen, just go in there with that burning righteous rage you showed me when I first started helping you. Don't lose your temper. You can *act* as if you've lost it and tempt him into doing something rash, but remember he'll be no walk-over." Gascon stopped. "This is always supposing you can get him alone without his bodyguard and force him into a fight."

"That's up to me." Alonzo nodded, "Well, my thanks to you, my friend. Are you sure you won't stand alongside me as my second?"

Gascon felt his eyes drop away from the earnest gaze of this intense young man. In a strange way, he was afraid. He never thought he would admit it to himself, but his two brushes with death after his duelling victory had scarred him and given him an awareness of his own mortality. When he was recuperating from the vicious beating as the Romany caravans trundled across Europe he had sworn he would never put his life on the line again.

"No, I'm sorry, Kosta. If I'm there as your second and you lose . . ." He let the rest of the sentence hang in mid-air, but Alonzo and Gordo read it right. All witnesses would have to be put to death if the Count

148

was the victor. No more to be said.

"I understand," the King said. "Don't feel bad. This is not your fight." He took a big breath, smiled, and trotted out an old Romany saying he had heard the women use: "Come, the sun stands high and there are fortunes to be read." He continued speaking in his mind "And Kingdoms to be won". And then, as an afterthought, he added, ". . . or lost!"

All the caravans had left the day before for the Fair, and now Turon and his trusty old horse Petro were on the move. Big Gordo sat astride the railings alongside Turon as he drove, and inside, taking no chances of being seen or recognised was the King himself.

They had made a round trip almost back to Grigori's old hut so that they would come in by another road altogether from the one the main body of Romanies had taken.

There had been a big conference two nights before and this plan was made. The Romanies stood to lose everything if the King's attempt came to naught, and it was discovered that they had been harbouring him, so Alonzo was to be spirited in under cover of darkness and left at the derelict old woodcutter's hut. He was to hide there during the second day of the Fair and then Turon and Gordo would join him secretly at midnight on the night before the ceremony and make their move.

Apparently the pottery figures found here and there in the castle during the previous month had done their work only too well. Bands of armed soldiers stopped every traveller into the city and security at the Palace was at a fierce level. Count Tzlenko was reported to have been apoplectic with rage when he had walked out of his bedchamber and stumbled over the last of them, the representation of the King delivering the killing thrust to a very recognisable Count. He was livid apparently, smashing the terracotta figures into tiny pieces, and then summoning the guard, at that early hour, to search the castle.

The capital was in a foment of intrigue and rumour. This person and that person claimed to have seen the King, or to know of his whereabouts, hoping to gain a little notoriety amongst his or her acquaintances. This sort of story-telling came to a rapid end when two such braggarts were arrested and put to the torturer to find out what they knew. After that, no more rumours were heard, but the mood of the people took a very decided turn against the Count and towards this legendary Alonzo, who was supposedly coming back from the dead, *and* in the not too distant future, to reclaim his throne.

It was against this knowledge that Turon's caravan crept in towards the castle on the pre-arranged track. Turon was alert, but he carried no light of any sort and in the early evening darkness the robbers were on him before he knew it. There was a fierce scuffling, a yell of "Kosta – out here!" and the boy was felled with a blow to the head.

Gordo had been dozing in the open doorway of the caravan. He came up, eyes starting out of his head, swinging the stool he had been sitting on. It connected with a sickening blow and one of the assailants was out of the fight, probably for good.

Gordo got his sword out, but was in an awkward spot

150

for doing much. Turon was slumped at his feet and the railings prevented him from using his sword to any good effect.

Luckily the attackers were no better placed, having to try and get to a man standing three steps above them, and for a while it was a stalemate, with every sword slash a wasted effort.

Suddenly there was a ghastly shriek and one of the attackers went slowly forward onto his knees, and then full out on his face, revealing the bearded Alonzo, sword wet in his hand. It had gone against the grain to attack unannounced from behind but, as Gascon had advised him, "In a life and death fight there are no niceties, no manners. It's kill or be killed!" The King had wriggled out of the little window at the rear of the caravan and sword in hand, had come upon the four assailants from behind.

It was far from over however.

Big Gordo had jumped down and was now laying about him with the stool, but it was obvious that the sword in his other hand would be no match for any of the three swords ranged against them. The friends manoeuvred themselves into a position where the caravan was at their back, and from there, in the half dark they did their best.

Luckily it was just as dark for the attackers and for a while no fancy sword-play was possible, but it soon became clear that it was only a matter of time before the three assailants conquered Alonzo and Gordo.

Suddenly there was a thundering of hooves. Alonzo snatched a sideways glance and his heart leapt as he recognised Gascon. The Corsican was out of the saddle in an instant, the riderless horse trotting on for a few more yards and then turning to watch, whites of the eyes huge in the darkness.

Now it was a different story. Three against three and Gascon a master. In a short space of time the man he had singled out was wounded and was away and running, his sword abandoned. Gordo's opponent turned briefly to see what was going on, but it was long enough for Gordo to connect with a round house swing that felled the man where he stood.

Gascon held the big man back when he would have gone to the King's aid. This fight was the very thing that Alonzo needed.

The sound of a horse departing the scene in haste indicated that Gascon's wounded man was making his escape, so all attention could now be focused on the struggle taking place before them.

Attack, parry, riposte, counter attack, on and on it went in one continuous movement. As the two watched, Gascon's expression slowly turned to one of contentment. Alonzo was obviously operating on two different levels. One was instinctive, based on all the work he had done over the past months, but the other level was one of constantly watching and assessing his opponent's patterns of fighting and looking ahead and planning his timing to take advantage of these patterns.

It became obvious to Gascon that his protégé had the upper hand, and had suddenly become aware of that fact himself.

They could see the subtle difference. Alonzo pretended to be having the worst of it, pretended to give ground, and suddenly it was all over. The Corsican's secret move had worked spectacularly. Alonzo stood white-faced, arms widespread, hands flicking as if they would rid themselves of the horror before him. His opponent lay dead.

Alonzo's legs gave way beneath him and Gascon was left with the task of removing the sword from the body.

"What changed your mind?" Alonzo croaked later. They had propped him against the caravan's wheel.

"I couldn't stop myself, Kosta. I saw you in trouble and the next thing I knew I was hard at it."

"No . . . I mean, what fortune brought you here when we needed you?"

The Corsican's face turned grim. "I was seeking you. I knew which way you were coming in, and when Silvander and Lissia were arrested, I . . . "

"What!?" The word shot out like a thunderclap from Gordo and Alonzo at exactly the same time. Gordo had the Corsican by the front of his jacket before he could think, "Lissia . . . what happened?"

"Let go, Gordo, for God's sake." The King lurched unsteadily to his feet. "Tell us quickly . . . what happened?"

Gascon explained. "Everybody set up their tents with all their wares on display and Silvander had one of your pottery portraits of him alongside his name, to attract customers, I suppose. Everyone knows him, and it's such a good likeness . . . "

"The fool!" Alonzo smashed his fist into the palm of his other hand in frustration. "Go on."

"Well, there's been such a furore about these terracotta figures of yours, and I suppose some spy

153

reported back to the Palace. Anyway, a detachment of soldiers came and the captain demanded to know who had made the figure. Before he could stop himself, Silvander, trying to protect you, said, 'my daughter', then he realised what he had said, tried to take it back and say it was himself and finally got really tongue-tied. The soldiers just bundled up the two of them and they were marched away, pottery figure with them."

"I'll kill the . . ."

"Shut up, Gordo!" Alonzo's voice sliced through the darkness. "We'll go in tonight! Could you shave me, Gascon? I couldn't trust myself. I'd probably cut my own throat." He laughed in a despairing sort of way.

"What do you want to shave for?"

"If I get to meet him face to face I want him to recognise me immediately . . . Are you coming with us, Gascon?"

There was a long silence, and finally the Corsican said, "What's the point of life if you don't do what you think is right?" He gave a huge sigh. "Yes . . . I'm with you."

They revived Turon with a slosh of water over his face, but he was in no condition to drive and so Gordo took over the reins.

The caravan, Gascon's horse tied to the back, moved off in the direction of the castle.

No one gave a second glance at the bodies, dead or unconscious, stretched out on the grass. The Corsican smiled to himself. His King had survived, and come through his "baptism of iron" with flying colours. It was just possible that this mad scheme might even work.

Alonzo's face was stinging. The ordeal of being shaved

by Gascon in the bumpy caravan would have been bad enough, but cold water and no soap at all had made the whole thing somewhat of an ordeal.

So it was that Alonzo was thinking more of the discomfort of his cheeks than of the job at hand and was completely unprepared for trouble to come from behind him.

Alonzo, Turon, Gascon and Gordo were in the secret tunnel, one small flickering torch the only light between them.

Turon was still feeling shaky. Big Gordo was bringing up the rear and so was not immediately missed. The first Alonzo knew of a problem was when a long, blood-curdling wail from the rear stood all the hairs up on the back of his neck.

"Shhh!" he hissed, spinning round. "What in God's name do you think you're playing at?"

Behind him he could just make out Gascon's worried face in the gloom.

"What is it?" he asked.

"Don't know. I can't see anything." The awful howling continued. They would surely be discovered if it kept up.

"Take the torch and lead the way back, quickly!" He passed the light to the Corsican and added, "Have your knife in hand."

"I already have!" Gascon set off carefully in the narrow tunnel with Alonzo right on his heels. It was impossible to pass one another in the confines of the passageway.

The noise got louder. It was a most terrible sound of someone in distress and suddenly they could make out

Turon and Gordo in the gloom. The noise was coming from the big man. He had Turon by both wrists in a grip of iron and his eyes were bulging from his head. He was plainly terrified. Turon was keeping up a steady flow of whispered instructions but none of them were reaching through to penetrate Gordo's terror.

"What's happened?" Alonzo tried to mix shouting and whispering.

Turon turned his head as much as he could to reply and it was really hard to hear him over the sound from Gordo.

"I came back to see and he grabbed me. He's hurting me, Kosta!"

"What started it?"

"I don't know."

All the time the hysterical wailing continued.

"Lean to your left." A sharp command from Gascon. Turon obeyed and the Corsican put everything he could into a wicked punch that caught the big Romany flush on the chin and the noise stopped. Blessed silence.

"Thank God for that!" Alonzo was sweating with fear. To have come all this way and have done all that training just to be caught now by a patrol of soldiers would have been too cruel.

The big man had half-collapsed and was virtually wedged in the narrow tunnel. He was making strange sobbing noises.

"He can't help it," Gascon said, "I've seen this sort of thing before. A man in my regiment, bravest soldier, could not stand being in an enclosed space. He was cashiered in disgrace for cowardice and nothing I said would they listen to. He'd been thrown in a tiny unlit cell

156

overnight after coming in drunk and he nearly went mad. Same howling. Sent shivers up my spine. Can I get past you somehow?"

Turon flattened himself against the stone wall and Alonzo took the torch as Gascon struggled to force his way past. It was a very difficult job but eventually Gascon was crouching face to face with the stunned Gordo.

The big man was whimpering, "I can't go on. It's pressing in on me. I'll be crushed. I can't breathe. I'm no use to . . ."

"Silence!" Gascon's military commanding voice cracked out and Gordo stopped in surprise.

"We need you, Gordo."

"I can't *bear* it! I've never felt anything like this in my life. I can't go on . . . I can't . . . I just can't." He was close to screaming pitch again as Gascon turned to talk past Turon to the King.

"Could you manage without the light?" he asked.

"Do it blindfold," the King replied without a moment's hesitation. "If you carry the light would it . . ." Gascon started to ask but the big man's voice was pitiful. "I can't, I can't. I must get out of here. Don't ask me."

"Gordo," Alonzo said quietly, "They've got Lissi. They'll torture her, kill her maybe to find out about the figures I made. We need you . . . Lissia needs you." There was a long silence while all their futures hung in the balance, and then Gordo took in a long shuddering breath, let it out again very shakily and said, "Give me the torch. I'll try," in a quavery voice.

It would have been laughable such a small voice coming from such a big man if the moment had not been so charged with tension. "Go as fast as you can," he said, "I'm on the edge of panic."

"Right!" Alonzo turned and was off into the familiar tunnel.

"Tell Gordo about the echo," he called back to Turon who was sticking to him like a shadow.

Turon called back over his shoulder to warn Gordo about the echo footsteps that had filled him with panic on *his* first tunnel trip, and somehow this helped to lessen his own fear.

All too soon they were at the steps, the circular stairway carved out of the rock by those clever stonemasons of so long ago and Gordo could neither move forward nor back. He was in real danger of being stuck.

His voice rose into a screaming wail and Gascon spun round and slapped him open-handed across the side of the face, then immediately moved in to give the big man a comradely hug and to whisper, "Lissia . . . do it for Lissia."

It was such an awkward situation, hemmed in on all sides by the living rock, Gascon a step above Gordo clutching him round the shoulders, but somehow the big man smothered his terror yet again, and sucking in huge gulps of air like a drowning man he managed to force his great bulk up the narrow stairs into the small chamber where Alonzo was already striking another light. The extra space seemed the height of luxury after the tunnel.

The four friends sank down onto the stone floor, all sweating profusely, and tried to smile reassuring smiles at one another.

"I'm sorry . . ." Gordo started but Gascon cut him off in mid-word.

"I salute you, Gordo. That took real courage. Make no apologies. We all admire you tremendously." And he nodded his head to give emphasis to the truth of what he said.

Gordo's eyes filled with tears and he squirmed miserably where he sat. "I've never in my – "

"Don't say anything," Alonzo murmured, "we're just so pleased you got through. We couldn't do it without

159

you. Right – plans. Now, the key. Where did I tell Roger to leave the key?"

He had deftly changed the subject and pretended a loss of memory just to give the big Romany some other problem to occupy his mind.

"Don't you remember? You said over in the old box there. Hide it *under* something you said." Turon chimed in, and then realised when he saw Alonzo's wink, that the King hadn't forgotten at all. The two friends exchanged a knowing look.

"Ah, now I recall," and the King moved over and opened the old chest. "Hey, look." He waved the others closer.

The opening lid revealed two uniforms and two helmets jammed into the small space. Two of them could disguise themselves as castle guards. It would take care of one tricky problem if a guard was posted at Count Tzlenko's door. Two of them would at least be able to get within sword range. "Roger, you're a marvel," he muttered.

They shook the uniforms out and tried to work out who could best wear them. It was a simple choice really – Gordo was out. He was far too big for either uniform, and Gascon said the King should not be involved as he would be too easily recognised with his beard shaved off.

So, Turon and Gascon got themselves all dressed in the uniform of the guard, the doublet and hose, the overjacket with the scallop sleeves and the belt and the iron helmet.

Turon's uniform looked a bit baggy on him, but in the dark it should be good enough to get him quite close to any real guard that was there.

Alonzo said a silent thank you to old Roger as he dug around looking for the duplicate key. When he finally found it, it looked such an amateurish job. It was unpolished, the marks of the file were all over it where it had been fine shaped, and Alonzo hoped that it would in fact open the Count's bedchamber door. If it didn't, they were lost.

No one had any idea of the time, but it was certainly well past the middle of the night when Alonzo trod down the stone release mechanism and the door cracked open a fraction and began to swing inwards. Gascon and Turon took several huge breaths and then pushed through the small gap into the dark of the Palace.

"Halt! Who goes there?"

"Relief guard," Gascon answered quietly, continuing to march forward. Turon was holding the flickering torch up slightly behind his head so that both their faces were in shadow.

"What are you doing coming from *that* direction? Who are you, anyway? Names?" This last statement was cracked out in a slightly panicky voice, and the two bogus guards heard the grating sound of swords loosening in scabbards with a sinking feeling.

"We've been checking the end of the corridor . . ." Gascon started, but the first guard jumped in, "You can't get down there without passing us. What the devil are you up to?" Both swords were out.

As arranged, Gascon and Turon had marched smartly past, just out of sword range, and the two guards turned, following them with the points of their weapons.

161

"Halt – stand still! What the devil do you think you're doing?"

Neither guard saw the huge figure of Gordo as he moved quickly and silently on bare feet behind them. The sound their helmets made as the big Romany banged their heads together would have set anyone's teeth on edge. It seemed so loud. Both helmets were dislodged and the men were turned by the scruff of the neck to face one another and once again their heads were bashed together from close range. Their swords clattered across the stone flagged corridor and it was all over.

The King came running up. "Good man!" He dropped Gordo's boots on the ground and slapped the Romany on the back. Then he fumbled to get the duplicate key into the lock. The guttering light in the sconces either side of the door cast eerie moving shadows everywhere.

"What do we do with these two beauties?" Gascon had doubled back with Turon, and was now looking down at the bloodied faces of the unconscious guards.

"Quiet!" The King was turning the key slowly and suddenly the door gave slightly. "It's worked!" Alonzo whispered excitedly. "We'd better drag them inside, out of sight of anyone."

He turned the big bronze handle and the door, creaking slightly, swung open. Turon followed the King as he stepped, sword now clear of his scabbard, into the bedchamber. The King's shadow moved huge and grotesque on the far wall, as he peered ahead to pierce the darkness.

His heart was thumping away in his chest. What would he find? Would his beloved Alice be here already sharing the Count's life? His mouth was dry as he threaded his way through the furniture across the huge carpeted room to the four poster bed. Behind the drawn curtains he could see the glow of a night light.

He was totally unaware of the guards being dragged in, of the door being closed and re-locked from the inside. Turon, standing behind him with the torch, could have easily been back at the camp or in another country altogether for that matter. The King's whole attention was focused on the bed as he took the curtain with the point of his rapier and inched it aside. He sucked a huge relieved breath as he saw the Count, alone, asleep beneath the sheets.

"Kill him now, Kosta!" Turon's voice shocked him. He turned his face to his friend and frowned.

"How could I live with myself?" he whispered. "No. Turon, you know me, I'm no fly-by-night cut throat. Go round and wake him." There was no "if you please", or "would you mind" from Alonzo now. He was the King in his own domain, giving orders to his loyal subject. There was no questioning that command.

Turon crossed to the other side of the bed, pulled the curtains back and tapped the Count twice where his shoulder bulged under the sheet.

Alonzo watched the slow waking process, the few snorted intakes of breath, marvelling at how insignificant the hated Count looked dressed in his nightcap with the tassel, his mouth slack and open.

"Come on, Turon . . . *wake* the man."

This time the Romany lad grasped the shoulder through the sheet and shook it until the Count awoke.

It could have looked almost comical, the way the

163

Count's eyes snapped open and his mouth clamped shut at practically the same instant, but there was nothing even vaguely amusing in the way the colour drained from his cheeks when he saw Alonzo, rapier in hand, at his bedside.

For the space of maybe three heartbeats everyone was frozen, seemingly waiting for someone else to make the first move.

"You!" the Count's voice was a croak, but it jerked him into action. He spun around and grabbed the tapestry bellpull by the bed and tugged furiously at it. There was no sound in the room, of course, but Alonzo knew that all these bellpulls connected to the servants' hall where, at this very moment, a numbered bell would be jangling furiously.

"Stop him! Stop him, Turon!" the King shouted. Turon seized the Count's arm, but was no match for the fanatical strength of the man. His efforts, in fact, were only helping to jerk the bellpull even harder.

Suddenly he let go of the arm, ducked down, and came up, dagger in hand to neatly sever the tapestry strip as high as he could reach. The Count crouched in the bed, the useless piece of the bellpull in his hand, breathing as heavily as if he had run up two flights of stairs.

"Get it over with," he snarled, "kill me."

"I will kill you when I am ready to kill you," Alonzo replied with as much venom in his voice as he could muster, and stepping forward he backhanded his enemy across the face with his left hand. "Consider yourself challenged to a duel."

The Count slowly wiped the trickle of blood from the corner of his mouth and stared coldly at Alonzo.

"You would match swords with *me*?" He laughed a short humourless laugh. "You're a dead man . . . your Majesty."

Once again Alonzo noted that pause, that deliberately insulting tone of voice, and his blood seemed to boil in his veins. He turned away to hide his fury and snapped back over his shoulder, "Get dressed." And added for good measure, "In whatever clothes you wish to be buried in. Watch him . . . he's a snake!" This last command was addressed to Gascon.

Big Gordo stood guard by the door and Alonzo moved over to be with him. He had no desire to see the Count changing out of his nightshirt. The thought disgusted him. *Everything* about the Count disgusted him. He would have to guard against losing his temper in the forthcoming fight to the death. "Keep cool," he kept saying to himself, "keep cool." He tried to calm his breathing. "Do something to occupy yourself," he thought.

"We should have company very soon," he said to Gordo. "Turn the key sideways in the lock so it can't be dislodged from the outside." A groan from the floor alerted him to another problem. What to do with the guards?

"Rip up the sheets and tie these fellows hands behind them. I don't want them entering the fight in the middle of things. Better tie their ankles together too for good measure." Big Gordo moved to carry out these instructions and Alonzo marvelled at how he himself had changed. Giving orders, and expecting them to be obeyed, seemed second nature to him suddenly.

There was a furious banging at the door and everyone

165

stopped dead in the bedchamber. "Count Tzlenko! Count Tzlenko! Are you all right?" a voice shouted. There was a long listening pause and then, "Count Tzlenko!" again. The door handle was tried to no avail. Alonzo could hear muttering going on and could distinguish a few phrases. "Where are the guards? Search . . ." and "Battering-ram party . . ." were two of the things he could make out. Then came the sound of someone running off down the corridor, followed by Count Tzlenko's sardonic voice behind him, "I await your pleasure . . . your Majesty."

Once again, that pause. The young King turned slowly to face his enemy and felt the cold jumping in the pit of his stomach as he realised what an imposing figure the Count made. Even unshaven and with his grey hair dragged back and tied in a hasty knot at the nape of his neck he still had an aura of command about him. He was dressed in a loose shirt open at the throat and belted pants tucked into soft leather boots and he seemed to tower over the wiry Corsican who was guarding him.

"Gordo – leave that for a minute and wedge something under that doorhandle, that heavy oak chair should do it. They'll try and batter the door down. Finish tying them up after you've done that and then the door is your problem – I don't want anyone coming in to disturb us. Is that clear?

Big Gordo was already dragging the chair across, and just nodded his agreement. The King turned back and faced his enemy's contemptuous gaze.

"Turon, you will act as second to this man. No argument! Gascon – you will be my second." He handed his rapier to Gascon. "Give him choice of weapons."

Turon stood holding the torch sullenly as Gascon laid his and Alonzo's rapier side by side over his arm, hilts facing the Count.

Tzlenko moved forward, never taking his eyes from the King's face and contemptuously took Alonzo's rapier. His mouth moved slowly into that sardonic smile as he slashed the rapier from side to side, testing its flexibility and enjoying the sound it made.

The King took Gascon's rapier as it was offered, tried to look as nonchalant as the Count, and failed. He felt ill at ease, almost the little boy in the man's world again. He must fight to conquer this. The rest of the furniture was cleared to one side. Gascon moved to a position behind him and the King breathed in deeply and said, "*En garde.*"

He heard his voice break slightly as he said it and once again the hated twin patches of red appeared on his cheeks.

The Count laughed, a short "huh" sound, at the sight of the King blushing and at that precise moment there was a shuddering crash from the door.

"Kosta!" Turon yelled and the King jerked his eyes back from the doorway to see the Count in a lightning fast lunge. Somehow he caught the big man's blade to deflect the killing blow but he was unprepared for the strength in the Count's wrist. He watched in horror as his sword was jerked from his hand and flipped end over end to land with a clatter against the wall.

The Count straightened up and with a grin like a death's head he came again. Alonzo had no other choice than to grasp and deflect the sword with his left hand. It saved his life but the forward and backward movement

167

of the rapier inside his clenched fingers seemed to burn a searing path through every nerve-ending in his body.

"Catch, Kosta!" Gordo, with lightning fast reflexes for such a big man, lofted one of the captive guard's swords and Alonzo was able to pick it out of the air in exactly the right position to parry the flurry of blows from the Count.

Tzlenko took pause, the smile gone, and Alonzo breathed again. His pulse was racing and thudding in his ears.

"No such luck on the next round . . . your Majesty."

This time the sneering tone of voice had no effect on the King. His left hand was throbbing and from the corner of his eye he could see the blood running back down his arm and soaking into the sleeve of his shirt, but nothing was going to distract him again in this fight. The continuous crashing of the battering-ram on the door became merely a background accompaniment to the action before him.

A lunge from the Count, parry and riposte from himself, marvel at the ease with which Tzlenko parried and moved back into the attack, then watch in quiet amazement as Gascon's lessons became second nature, instinctive almost. All those hours in the tent were paying off.

Alonzo started to settle into a routine, realised the trap here and altered his attack from *sixte* to *septieme* the next time, then *quarte,* then *quarte* again. He started to feel very good and began trying to manouevre the Count into pieces of furniture around the room.

The Count stopped, slashed his rapier from side to side, hoping the sound would unnerve his opponent, but

168

Alonzo lunged and lunged again and suddenly the Count was caught unprepared. He barely avoided the final probing move as he jumped awkwardly backwards, fetched up against the wall and frantically fought his way out of trouble. There was a large gash in his shirt, and the trickle of red from his chest underneath attested to the closeness of the King's attack.

There was a new awareness in the Count's eyes. This would be no easy win, no mis-match between unequal talents. One could almost see him stiffening his resolve before he launched into a new fury of attack. Back and forth they raged, the click and slash and slither of iron blade against iron blade a teeth-grating sound.

There was a splintering crash from behind and a yell from Gordo, a great clamour of voices from outside and another crash as the iron head of the battering-ram finally smashed its way through the door.

Somehow the King kept his attention to his front and with a quickening of the pulse felt his blade being engaged and put into the awaited "bind" by his enemy. He watched it happening. It was almost as if someone else was operating his arms and legs. With practised ease he took the strength and power of the Count's blade and arm, and "allowed" himself to give ground. Just slightly to the left of his chest he watched the tip move until it was beyond doing him any harm.

Alonzo had been aware at all times of where the point of his own blade was in relation to his enemy's body and now it was only a matter of tilting it up and selecting the spot on the Count's chest as Tzlenko, mistakenly assuming he had the advantage, continued forwards.

Slowly, slowly, it seemed, the rapier entered the already reddened gash in the shirt front and even more slowly the King straightened his arm.

Count Tzlenko fetched up almost nose to nose with the King, a look of shocked surprise on his face. The pose of the two adversaries was almost a carbon copy of Alonzo's pottery figures. The Count's sword arm wilted and his rapier point lowered to the ground. Alonzo could feel Tzlenko's guard as it slowly slid down the length of his left thigh.

"*Touché* . . . your Majesty." The Count's last ghastly attempt at sardonic humour was marred by the blood that filled his mouth and overflowed to run down his chin. His eyes slowly seemed to dim and lose focus and the King stepped back and tried to remove his rapier.

Count Tzlenko's body sagged forward onto its knees as the King lifted his right foot, placed his boot square in the middle of his enemy's chest and pushed and pulled at the same time. The rapier slid out and the body folded slowly from the knees to collapse and slew sideways. Alonzo thought how small the man looked in death.

He became aware of the noise and movement all around him again and realised that all this had been shut off by the sharpening of his own senses in the last moments.

"The Count is dead! Long live King Alonzo IV!" Big Gordo's bellow shocked and silenced them all on both sides of the door.

"Long live King Alonzo IV!" Turon and Gascon shouted and faces were crowding to look through the shattered door at the four men unashamedly embracing and slapping each other's backs.

There seemed no after effects this time. Alonzo's heart was still racing in his chest. He bent down and with his good right hand he closed the lids over the dead Count's staring eyes. He straightened up and to his amazement, his legs still supported him. He turned and to no one in particular he murmured, "Grigori . . . I avenge you."

A picture flashed into his mind of the old man, the coat and ginger wig in place, the eyes filled with tears and the marvellous smile. What a long time ago it all was.

"It *is* the King," someone whispered from outside the door, and then, "Long live King Alonzo IV," in a tentative sort of way, to be followed by a shout from everybody both inside and outside the chamber.

"LONG LIVE KING ALONZO IV!"

10

"You were great, Kosta," Turon chuckled, as he and Gascon moved forward again to grab the King in another bear hug.

"Not now. Guard your tongue. I'm the *King*, remember. Later – when we're alone." These words were hissed almost out of the side of Alonzo's mouth and Gascon, and Turon particularly, looked as if they'd been hit in the face with a bucket of freezing water. There was no time for niceties or considering bruised feelings. Everything hung in the balance. The King turned to Gordo.

"Unlock the door. Untie these two guards. Who's in charge out there?"

"I am, your Majesty." A face appeared in the middle of the crowd seen awkwardly through the smashed doorway.

"Name and rank!" snapped the King. He was enjoying this play acting.

"De Groot, Captain de Groot, Sir. Captain of the Guard."

"Fetch my wife."

"She's in the cells, Sir."

"She's WHAT?" Alonzo's voice shook the walls.

"Count's orders, Sir, she was to be held there until the wedding."

"The Count is no longer giving orders . . . as you can see." Alonzo's voice was quiet and cold in its menace. Everyone felt the iron behind the velvet tone.

"Fetch my wife to me and pity help anyone who has harmed her. Summon Roger and have him bring a surgeon. And there were two Romanies brought in for questioning yesterday, an old man, white beard, hook nose, and his daughter. Have them brought to me as well." The Captain stood at attention and Alonzo snapped, "Jump to it!"

"Sir!" The Captain saluted, turned and actually ran down the corridor.

"Who is next in command?"

"I am, Sir, Corporal Brattner, Sir." The man snapped to attention his sword at the "present" position, thumb touching his nose.

"Have these two men medically attended to and alert the Palace that I will have an audience in the throne room at . . . what o'clock is it?"

"It must be after four, your Highness." The Corporal replied.

"Audience will be at nine o'clock sharp. You will conduct me to my own quarters and bring my wife and the other prisoners there when they arrive."

*   *   *

The door closed and the King relaxed. It was wonderful to be in his own quarters once again. He turned and looked at the three Romanies standing awkwardly, ill at ease in this grand room.

175

"Well," he said, smiling to ease the frosty atmosphere, "we did it, I don't think I believed we could, you know. Without you three I never would have done it . . . Come on, cheer up . . . Turon."

"We don't know where we are with you, Kosta," the Romany lad murmured sullenly. "Blow hot, blow cold. One minute you silence us like a trio of peasants and the next, you expect us to be blood brothers again. We don't know how you expect us to act."

Alonzo strode straight across and enfolded the Romany boy in a huge bear hug.

"Turon, you've saved my life . . . I don't know how many times. You were the only one to believe my ridiculous tale of kings and castles. *You* showed me how to act in the Romany world. I know how *this* old world ticks. I'm the *King!* Any show of weakness or of me being like an ordinary commoner back there, and those soldiers would probably have killed us all. When we're alone we're just as we are . . . four good friends. When anyone else is observing us we must behave the way they expect us to behave. We must be as King and subjects . . . just until I have established myself firmly back in place . . . Is that a deal?"

The four men looked at one another, the smiles spread on the faces and hands were clasped and backs slapped.

"A deal!" they smiled.

A knocking on the door startled them.

Alonzo said, "Quickly – King and subjects – just to impress the others . . . quickly, stand over there . . . Come!"

The door opened and Alonzo gasped as he saw his

176

wife. She looked awful. She had the pallor of a life prisoner and dark rings of tiredness under her eyes as if they had been painted on. Her hair was all tangled.

"Alice!" The King held his arms out and watched the incredulous look take over her face.

"He told me you were dead. My God, Alonzo, I thought you dead all this time." She began to walk to him, but her limbs went slack and her eyes turned up in her head.

Alonzo had to jump to catch her and the pair of them went down in an untidy heap on the carpet.

"Help me," the King shouted. He had seen the three friends move to help, and had tried to make it look as if he had ordered them to do so. They exchanged knowing looks. "This King stuff will take some getting used to," Turon thought. Together they carried the unconscious young Queen and laid her on the bed and it was only when the King had come back to demand that ladies-in-waiting be sent for, that he saw Silvander and Lissia standing surrounded by soldiers.

"What's this?" he demanded.

"You ordered me to bring these two prisoners for questioning, Sir," Captain de Groot replied.

"You misunderstood me, Captain. I ordered you to bring them to me, but not for questioning. Release them immediately."

"Yes, your Majesty. Forgive me, Sir, my misunderstanding. I thought . . ."

"Say no more." The King cut him off in mid-sentence. He watched as bonds were untied from wrists and then formally welcomed Silvander and his daughter. Their look of surprised distrust would have been comical had the King been able to relax and laugh, but there were too many watching.

"As soon as Roger and the surgeon arrive, bring them in. Meanwhile close the door. Oh . . . the same for the ladies-in-waiting. Bring them in here too. Have a runner standing by for any messages I want delivered. That will be all."

"Your Majesty." Captain de Groot saluted and quietly closed the door.

Alonzo shook off the "King" pose and turned to the silent group of Romanies.

"It's really me" he said, "Lissi, Silvander, we *did* it! Tzlenko is dead. We came a day early to rescue you. Are you harmed?"

Lissia stood looking at the young King. "No," she said in a small voice. How handsome he looked, and how she envied the Queen her pale and illtreated "interesting" look. She could not believe it when they had all three been marched up from the cells together. She had seemed to know instinctively that this was his Queen. How could she, a Romany maid, ever have hoped to compete? She turned and held out her arms to the big Romany. "Gordo . . . I never thought to see you again." The big man plunged across the room and swept her into his arms.

"Lissi . . . Oh Lissi," he mumbled into her hair.

Alonzo felt a brief stab of jealousy.

"I nearly killed us all," Silvander said, "I never thought. I'm sorry. What of your hand, my son?" His look of concern warmed Alonzo.

"I have the surgeon coming to look at it," he said, "Are *you* all right?"

"They were leaving us to stew overnight with a promise of the torturer this morning if we told them nothing. I don't know how I would have stood up under that . . ." Silvander left it in mid air as Alonzo took him by the shoulders and gave him a huge hug.

* * *

The throne room was crowded. It was well after nine and the buzz of voices was everywhere. Half the Romany camp was there, roused from their sleep by the soldiers, and escorted to the castle protesting their innocence. Ordinary folk from all walks of life were there – dignitaries summoned from their first meal of the day – market traders, in fact a good cross section of the people making up the capital. The huge double doors at the entrance facing the throne were open, and newcomers continued to jam into the antechamber.

The hastily written proclamations posted on the main castle walls and the town criers had done their job.

Something was happening. The blanket sound of voices dropped to a hush of expectancy as the beautifully clad Major Domo moved into the centre of the room, slammed down his staff of office three times and raised his voice in the ensuing silence:

"King Alonzo IV and Queen Alice! Long live the King and Queen!"

"Long live the King and Queen!" the crowd repeated dutifully and immediately there was a buzz of interest and whispered comment as the pair entered.

Alonzo's splendid appearance was marred slightly by the bandage on his left hand, but Queen Alice looked exquisite.

No one present in the audience would have been aware of the amount of work needed to cover her prison pallor or the work put in by the tailors to take in the King's clothes to fit his new trim shape. They made a fine pair.

As soon as they were seated on the thrones on the dais, the young King rose to his feet once more.

"You see before you a changed King." He cleared his throat. "In the middle of last year I suffered an assassination attempt."

180

A buzz of conversation swept round the room and out into the crowded antechamber. The King waited until the sound had died down, and continued.

"The author of that plan to foully murder me was my former Prince Regent, the Count Tzlenko, who used his position . . ." the King was unable to continue over the uproar in both rooms.

"Silence! Silence for your *King!*" the Major Domo shouted, and his huge staff plunged up and down banging on the floor to restore order.

"I have this very day released my wife, the Queen, from the dungeons, where she was held as a common prisoner awaiting the time, not too far distant, when she was to be forced into a mockery of a marriage with this man."

The low outraged murmur from the crowd was now a constant background to the speech. The King raised his voice somewhat and continued.

"In the early hours of this morning, I was forced by circumstances to creep, like a thief, into my own Palace to confront the Count. I challenged him to a duel." The King paused for dramatic effect, and was inwardly revelling at being so effectively the centre of attention. He swept the room with his eyes, trying to meet every glance, both in the throne room and in the room beyond. He began again.

"You see before you the victor, wounded slightly," here he briefly raised his bandaged hand, "but none the less the victor." A long pause, enjoying the silence, and then, "The Count paid the ultimate price. Those of you who wish to convince yourself that this all powerful, evil man is no longer with us, can view his earthly remains which will be on show for the rest of this day on a slab outside the prison gates." The King carried on, raising his voice again to ride over the murmuring from all sides.

"I have today ordered the clearing of the castle dungeons." A ragged cheer started and soon the sound was deafening. No amount of thumping and shouting from the Major Domo had any effect. Finally it was the King who restored order by simply raising both hands high in the air.

"I would re-start my reign afresh. Henceforth there will be no imprisonment without trial . . ." He stopped the rising cheer once again by raising his hands. "Hear me out. Prisoners of Count Tzlenko are free to appeal against wrongful imprisonment and just compensation will be paid . . . in GOLD COIN!"

Alonzo shouted out the last two words and sat down. The tumult in the throne room and in the antechamber was indescribable. Every face seemed wreathed in smiles. The market trading fraternity were clapping each other on the back with excitement. The King reached across with his good hand and held his beloved Alice's hands briefly, exchanging such a look of love and adoration. He turned to the front, took a deep breath and stood once again. The silence was instant.

"I summoned the treasurer from his bed early this morning," a ripple of laughter went round the rooms. "He was not best pleased!" Again the laugh.

"We had discussions and now see eye to eye, and, as I think you have guessed, I am taking my Kingdom back onto the gold standard!"

The uproar was instant and enormous. The King

shouted, "Master Treasurer!" A studious looking man stepped forward, a sheaf of papers in his hands. Alonzo sat down heavily. Exhaustion was not far away. It had been a long, long night.

The treasurer had every ear as he droned on and on, detailing the arrangements for exchanging the paper money for gold and silver coin once again. He was an unutterably boring speaker, and when Queen Alice brushed the King's arm with a butterfly light touch, he realised with a jolt that he was on the verge of nodding off. He shook his head, and lurched to his feet once again.

"Forgive me," he laughed, "I'm exhausted. It's not every day one recaptures one's Kingdom." The good natured crowd laughed with him.

"Have you touched on taxes?" he called after the departing treasurer. The man stopped, turned and shook his head, looking at the King over the tiny glasses perched on the end of his nose.

"We have discovered, this morning, between us," the King nodded, dismissing the treasurer with a gesture of his hand, "that the Count had been systematically robbing the country over the past several years, even before my own father, the late King, died. There are enormous sums of money due, most of which are recoverable, I understand." Here he exchanged a nod of agreement with the departing treasurer.

"These monies will go into the exchequer and once the financial situation has been examined, I think I can safely promise you a further huge cut in taxes." A great cheer rocked the rooms.

The King sat and beckoned the Major Domo. A hasty

whispered consultation was held and the Major Domo then straightened, banged his staff three times on the floor and intoned, "Bring forth the Sword of State!" The cry was repeated through the corridors and eventually a footman appeared, flanked on both sides by members of the castle guard. He was carrying a silken cushion upon which lay the beautifully worked Sword of State in the equally finely chased gold and silver scabbard.

The King stood up again. He was exhausted now, but a few more formalities to be gone through and he felt he could sleep forever. He cleared his throat, shook his head and began.

"In the past half a year I have been a man in hiding, going in fear of my life. During that time I have lived in the care and protection of the Romany community. I will never forget the debt I owe them. They not only saved my life, literally, but they were responsible for making a man of me. I would like you to welcome the Romany leader, the Shero Rom. Please join me." This last to the flustered old man who stood nervously smoothing his huge moustache with both hands.

The King held out his arms and said, "Come . . . you are among friends."

The old man tugged his jacket down on both sides, smoothed his shirt front and hesitantly walked forward. Alonzo moved to meet him, helped him up onto the dais and said quietly, just for the two of them to hear, "As you see, I lied. I *could* afford *several* swords." They exchanged smiles and suddenly there was a twinkle in the old Romany's eyes. The King flung his arms around the old man in a huge embrace.

"Welcome this marvellous man as you would welcome

184

your King," Alonzo shouted. "He gave me back my *life!*" Alonzo was stunned to see a blush mounting up the old man's cheeks. He laughed out loud with pleasure and joined in the spontaneous cheering.

"It would be an honour if your son Orlando would join us," Alonzo said, after the cheering had died down somewhat.

The Shero Rom turned and beckoned to his son, and Orlando, overcome by surprise forgot to scowl for once. He shouldered his way through to the front of the crowd and half-heartedly joined in with the hug that Alonzo offered. He was out of his depth in these surroundings.

"You are both most welcome," the King said quietly and sincerely, "I'm sorry I sent soldiers for you. I didn't know how else to make sure of your presence here today." He raised his voice, addressing the crowd once again.

"I have one final duty . . . well, pleasure really, before you can all go about your business. I would honour some men who have helped me hugely with no thought of reward. Send for Gordo Tirenac!"

Cries of "Gordo Tirenac" echoed in the corridor and the big man, red-faced, appeared, darting nervous glances in every direction. He moved forward as the King beckoned him and finally knelt on one knee when ordered to do so. The King took the glittering sword out of its scabbard and intoned in as powerful a voice as he could manage:

"For indispensable services to his King in the regaining of his rightful Kingdom." Here he ceremoniously touched Gordo's left and right shoulder with the flat of the sword. "Arise, Sir Gordo!"

185

The huge man stood up, blushing fluriously, and the King whispered, "Stand by me, Gordo . . . my friend." Then turning he whispered once again to the Major Domo.

This worthy cried out, "Send for Gascon de Severigny!" and presently the slight figure of the swordsman appeared, his military bearing making him look much taller.

"Ladies and gentlemen, look well on this man. This patient, clever man took me as a spoilt child and made me into a swordsman. Without his constant work and his inspirational knowledge and new ideas, it would be me lying on the slab there today."

Alonzo turned to Gascon. "I owe you more than I can ever express my friend," he said. "I would form a new academy of swordsmanship here in the Capital, with you at its head, on a full time or a part time basis. We can talk of this later, meanwhile please kneel facing me." Gascon smiled as he did so, and the King repeated the process with the sword, finishing with, "Arise, Sir Gascon!" The Corsican stood up and moved to the spot Alonzo indicated alongside Gordo, while the King turned and called to the Major Domo, "Send for Turon Repecharz!"

"Send for Turon Repecharz!"

"Turon Repecharz!" echoed in the hallways and corridors and Alonzo stood smiling a welcome as the young Romany came nervously into the huge room. There was such a lost look about him that Alonzo held out both arms and clasped the lad to him.

"What shall I say of this man?" Alonzo looked long into Turon's eyes. "Without his belief in me I would have been lost. He is some five or six years younger than I am, and yet, in wordly experience he was like a father to me. He has saved my life directly or indirectly so many times that I have lost count. With your permission, my subjects, I would appoint this man companion to the King and permanent advisor to the Crown on all things to do with the Romany Community. I would have him as direct liaison betwen your King and the Shero Rom." Alonzo looked questioningly at the old Romany leader who exchanged a glance with Orlando and then turned back and nodded his agreement to the King.

Alonzo's eyes centred on Turon once again. "I am creating a new hereditary title, to be passed down to your sons and their sons after them," he said, and added almost in what appeared as an afterthought, "Lord Turon." The Romany's mouth dropped open and his eyes filled with tears as the King clasped his shoulders and smiled at him.

They stood staring at each other for several moments and then the King seemed to shake himself awake.

"Can you bear with me for three more announcements?" he asked his subjects, and not waiting for any answer he cried, "Summon Silvander and Lissia Dajno, and Roger Dutz." The names were called and the Romany and his daughter were ushered into the room followed by old Roger.

The King spoke first to the potter. "You truly treated me as a son when I was almost friendless. I would like to continue that relationship now if you will have me as that son still?"

Silvander nodded, unable to trust his voice, and the

King continued, "You will always regard my home as your home – no formality – no ceremony," he raised his voice and directed his statement to everyone within earshot. "This man will be treated with all honour, courtesy and kindness due to a loved father, for that is how I regard him. Is that clear?"

There was a warm murmur of agreement from the assembled multitude and Alonzo smiled. He then held out his hands to old Roger.

"I think I've told you my feelings for you, my dear and faithful servant. During my childhood the only love and affection I knew was from you. I thought you were of a different breed, a different race almost, from every

other person in the Royal Court. I would have you retire on a full and generous pension . . ." He watched the old man shaking his head vigorously and said, "Would you rather stay on?"

"I should die within the year, my Lord, if I did not have your welfare constantly before me. All these months I thought you dead. It would be too cruel, now that you're back with us, if I were not able to serve you. I want no other reward," he whispered.

"So be it," said the King. "I declare this man a Freeman of the City and my body servant for as long as he wishes to be." He stopped, looking long and lovingly at the old man.

Dear Roger, he thought, *if you only knew how much I love you.* Slowly Alonzo turned and focused his attention on Lissia.

"And you . . . what shall I say to you, sweet girl? Were I a single man I would doubtless be fighting your betrothed for your hand." He exchanged a laugh with big Gordo but there were at least three, possibly four people there who sensed the truth and sincerity behind the apparently light-hearted banter.

"There is a huge wedding planned for two days hence. I would use the occasion to re-affirm my vows to my beloved Queen, a sort of second wedding. What say you, my love? Will you have me again?"

"Willingly, my Lord." Alice was on her feet and gravely moving to join her man. Alonzo took her by the hand and turned to big Gordo, "If you and your betrothed are of a like mind, Sir Gordo, I would love it to be a double ceremony."

He watched the looks between Lissia and Gordo, and Silvander and Lissia, and smiled.

"So be it," he said. "Now, one final thing before I fall into bed for several days of rest . . ." His voice half-broke and he giggled in a slightly hysterical way. He was really exhausted.

"In recognition of the hospitality of the Romanies I hereby absolve them from all taxes henceforth and in perpetuity . . ." There was an excited uproar from all sides. "I would also appoint them providers of honey to the Crown, if they feel that they can fulfil that position . . ." The image of old Grigori flashed before his eyes. "Perhaps next year? . . . We shall see . . . but now, on a final, more serious note . . . You all thought King Alonzo IV to be dead. I would leave it that way." There was a puzzled murmur from the assembly.

"In honour of the Romanies and as a gesture of thanks to them all, I take the name given to me in fun by the Romany children, my friends. Henceforth I will be known as King Kosta the First!"

Everyone was standing cheering, waving, and only Alonzo and his Queen heard Turon's light-hearted statement, "I preferred Cockroach . . . your Majesty."

He ducked to avoid a hastily aimed friendly swipe and the two men burst into laughter.

Dedication

It was in 1969 when, guided by naturalists Harry Butler and Vin and Carol Serventy, we made the television series 'Rolf's Walkabout' in the Northern Territory of Australia for the A.B.C. (Later shown several times on B.B.C.) Also on the trip and very much involved in the filming, was my wife Alwen, our five year old daughter, Bindi, and the Serventy children, Natasha (13), Cathy (11) and Matthew (5). Every night it became a ritual that I would create a new episode of an ongoing bedtime story to keep the children amused, and that's how this novel started.

I'm sure the story would have faded into oblivion had it not been for my breaking a journey to Bournemouth in 1975 by dropping in to see a pottery at Angel Farm in Lyndhurst. It was run by Joanna Witney and I was made very welcome by her and by her parents, and her father Roland, a retired farmer, captivated me then, and on subsequent visits, by holding forth on the subject of bees.

The insight he gave me into their habits and the way they regulate their lives was inspirational. That meeting and those visits to the farm and the pottery started me re-thinking my story in which both bees and pottery-making were key ingredients. I can remember thinking, 'If ever I write that yarn I'll get a tape recorder and sit down with this marvellous man and make sure I get all the facts right.'

Unfortunately, by the time I finally decided to do something about it, well into the eighties, Roland Witney had died, but to him, and to those delightful children who were such good listeners as we 'walked-about' the Top End of Australia, I dedicate this book.